# The Patron Saint
# of Lost Girls

## Maureen Aitken

# The Patron Saint of
# Lost Girls

Maureen Aitken

Southeast Missouri State University Press | 2018

*The Patron Saint of Lost Girls* by Maureen Aitken

Copyright 2018: Maureen Aitken

Softcover: $18.00

First published in 2018 by
Southeast Missouri State University Press
One University Plaza, MS 2650
Cape Girardeau, MO 63701
www.semopress.com

Cover Design: John Ilg
Author Photo: Tim Thayer

Library of Congress Cataloging-in-Publication Data

Name: Aitken, Maureen author.
Title: Patron saint of lost girls / by Maureen Aitken.
Description: Cape Giradeau : Southeast Missouri State University Press, 2018.
Identifiers: LCCN 2018009636 | ISBN 9780997926279
Subjects: LCSH: Women--Violence against--Fiction. | Women--Crimes against--Fiction. | Family life--Fiction. | City and town life--Michigan--Detroit--Fiction.
Classification: LCC PS3601.I87 P38 2018 | DDC 813/.6--dc23
LC record available at https://lccn.loc.gov/2018009636

*For Mary and Mary Ann Aitken*

# Table of Contents

# This is Art

IN AUGUST, WHEN the cicadas burned and the lawnmowers sounded like industrial bees, we couldn't stop. In the bedroom, on the couch, on the floor. Afterward we would lie there, reading the paper or letting the television taunt us like a car salesman. Paul would wiggle his toes against mine, and we'd look at one another for a long time. His face was like a catcher's mitt, warm and beaten. He reminded me of one of those boys who had moved away when I was little, but Paul had returned a man.

Then it would start all over again, and I felt like one of those cicadas, burning up from something that had no name. The dog licked our legs. The mail fell through the slot. But we didn't move. Even a smile felt like it would slice through us.

I don't know if we were fragile or potent or both, but one conversation dangled on us like an ornament. On a rainy and bruised July day, after Paul got off the phone with his father, I found him in a frozen stare, petting the dog.

"What's wrong?" I asked.

"He says it won't last, that nothing I do lasts more than a few months."

Then, as quickly as it arrived, Paul took a deep breath and said, "Fuck it." He didn't look afraid or worried or any of those other emotions that could be clicked back into joint.

He reached his arms out for me. I sat down wanting some explanation.

"That's crazy, right?"

"Don't worry. It's nothing."

But it was something, an accusation, a cruelty leveled upon us. Why didn't Paul defend us? He put his palm on my arm, and his sultry energy seared into me again.

We weren't crazy at first. We met at the Detroit Institute of Arts, where his company had farmed him out to do some on-site design. I worked for a curator named Bruno, who spoke four languages and kept long hours.

"These artists dedicated their lives to this work," Bruno said. "We won't let them down."

I knew from the start Paul wouldn't stay long. He was tall and twenty-six, and he used to throw paper airplanes on my desk. The image of his big fists folding the paper carefully and adjusting the nose point broke my heart a little. He wrote notes inside the airplanes: "You work too hard" and "Your boss is a jerk." He took nothing seriously, which meant the secretaries adored him. One after another asked, "So, do you paint?"

He thought they were all obnoxious, and told me so on our first date. We went to art movies—Jarmusch and Fellini. When I looked at the screen, I could see him there, riding through on the mystery train.

Nothing really happened on our first three dates. My neighbor across the hall, Mr. Jackson said, "You're dating again, I see."

I answered honestly. "He's a friend."

Mr. Jackson sniffed. "Watch yourself. He's a good-time Charlie."

"You should know. You wrote the book."

He laughed.

On the fourth date, Paul and I drank fishbowl margaritas and mocked Bruno's declarations. We picked up salt shakers, forks, and pennies off the table and said, "Now *this* is art." Under the table, all the while, I pressed my heel into my leg and thought this is what it feels like. If you fall for someone enigmatic, this is what you get.

Paul just wanted to be friends, I decided then. Friends were good, especially friends who could lift things. I didn't have one of those. As soon as I thought that, he leaned over and kissed me. We were at a table outside, our margarita glasses licked clean of salt, and I felt as though something enormous had just swept through town. Time seemed to lift, like a needle off an old record. It was June.

In a week, we fell in love, and in four, Paul moved in.

Mr. Jackson was always nice to Paul and then he'd smile at me with that expression, like, *You'll learn.*

On Monday mornings, we left the couch and the floor and the dog with that tilted, "Where are you going?" look. I drove to my job at the institute, and Paul went back downtown, to the main computer graphics shop where he would be farmed out again for a week or two. Most days he would call and say things like, "I cleaned all the spots off the Chevy Blazers" or "I'm creating mountains. I'm putting a Ram truck in the Himalayas."

He didn't mention his father's prediction. I didn't remind him. I thought of October, when the leaves would look like paintings, and I'd be able to say his father was wrong.

Bruno had a laundry list of duties: prep the slides for the Kandinsky show and run through the October exhibit with the theme, *Love in Dangerous Times.*

My job title was "assistant to the curator." Mostly it meant driving around in Bruno's Benz and answering calls from him. "Oh, Mary, could you swing by the Michigan Gallery and pick up a package waiting for us?" and "Mary, could you run out to the library and pick up some articles on Lichtenstein? We need them for the blurb."

I loved the smell of the leather seats and being outside. I used to drive the Benz down to see a couple of painter friends, Jan and Carl, so they could point and laugh, then flip me the bird.

I'd always loved the old bay windows and brick of houses on that street. In the Benz, though, I was reminded of the exhausted roofs and the rusty metal porch chairs. It was like someone telling you your mother was ugly, and for one frightening second you believed her. But I still liked the joke of rolling up in the Benz.

Sometimes Jan and Carl would walk downstairs, and if they didn't have any paint on them, we'd drive around, or maybe I'd drop them downtown. On the way Carl would say, "So when are you going to put one of my paintings in your swanky institute?"

One time Jan said, "Take us to a fancy spot." So I drove and drove, past the apartments and the little bars and the big business buildings where you couldn't park for all the people.

Finally, we reached the Whitney, a pink-stone restaurant with white lights like stars, even in the day. The valet came up and tried to open the door, but I lowered the window. "Can we just sit here?"

"Hey," the valet said, leaning in. "That you, man?"

"Yeah," Carl replied. They pressed their flat palms together and then slid them back.

"You're rolling now." The valet nodded, held up two fingers, and mouthed the word "peace" before a BMW drove up and he fell back into his official role.

We watched his face stiffen. His hand moved out gently to open the car door. "Good afternoon." We sat for a minute. A quiet fell over us, and it wasn't a joke anymore.

"I like our street better," Jan said. "Let's walk home."

"Yeah, good idea," Carl agreed. "Don't forget about the institute, Mary." He pounded his chest. "Get me while I'm cheap."

Sometimes I would drive around alone and think about Paul. He wouldn't be the first guy to leave. They gave their reasons. And if that had been the end I would have been fine with it. But too often, when the heartache eased, like the swell off a sprain, I'd get a phone call from the ex. It was always the same:

"Can we talk?"

"Sure."

"I miss you."

"No, you don't. You didn't want me. You weren't happy."

"No. I was happy. I fucked up. I was happy."

So I would run down the litany of bummers, like the beads on a rosary, things I told myself when they first left. "I didn't like your friends. I didn't ski. I didn't know what to say to people at parties. We liked different music. We fought."

The answer would always come back: "They were just parties."

I would blurt out what I didn't even know was true until that moment: "It's over."

After saying goodbye, I turned off the ringer. People threw people away. I couldn't fix that.

It was late when I got back. Bruno said, "The café is closed. Could you pick up some food? Anywhere. I'm starving. You know what I like, no fast food."

I got in the car and drove. All I saw were closed things, what used to be the burger joint next to the shell of the old Chinese place. Then an open Burger King, a Kentucky Fried Chicken. In the distance, the abandoned buildings and the fast food places resembled telephone poles or stop signs that repeated at the same intervals until the eye could no longer see them. What a weird knowledge, to understand that they carried on beyond my view, across the country. For every three miles, a McDonald's, for every exit, an order. To think of it wore me out, the way the view went on across the country, out past my wildest imagination. I found a parking spot in front of the falafel place.

After work, I took a shower and sat on our wooden porch shucking corn. I wore a violet dress my mother had given me. If a couple of its holes seemed unfashionable, it was tender. I felt the wood on my feet, and the day bled out of me.

Paul came home with his sunglasses half down his nose. He put his palm on my arm, and then walked upstairs to take a shower. Sometimes I felt as though we were living two lives—one of coffee in white mugs and central air, and the other with open windows, sirens, and floors worn from our passing.

Paul came out and put his arm around me. "Steak?"

"Chicken."

His face fell a little, but then I added, "Barbecue," and he brightened.

The prediction of our end, the denial, the avoidance, pressed heavier against us. The dog whined to be let out.

After dinner, we sat on the porch again. "They don't want Blazers on mountaintops," he said. "They want them on the moon now. Earth isn't good enough anymore."

I stared ahead at a neighbor, Betty, walking her dog. "You're bitter."

He turned and looked at me. "Bitter?" He looked down the road that dead-ended. "Compared to what?"

"You complain about your job, and yet you stay there. If you hate it, fix it."

Mr. Jackson walked up the steps with a wicker basket of kale and cabbage he'd cut from the garden. Once he'd passed, Paul said, "Right, I'll just go out and get a full-time job."

It was a recession. A lot of people worked part time. I knew that.

"Look, my grandfather was a coal miner," I said. "I try. I have to try."

Paul got up and walked inside. Because I still wanted him, I let him be.

When night came, his sullen nature turned the rooms gray. We lay on the couch watching sitcoms that weren't funny. He kissed my shoulder, steady and distant.

In the morning, the dog watched us leave with his curious expression. We held hands on the way out to our cars.

"Have a good day," I said.

"Yeah."

We kissed and walked our separate ways, our fingers slow to separate.

As I drove, the road looked cold. I couldn't find a free parking space, so I gave the attendant my five dollars. I don't know why I drove. It was only half a mile. I looked at the white stone Institute with the purple film society sign and a Cadillac parked in front.

Bruno didn't have any errands for me. All day we organized slides for the exhibit. We moved Lange's *Migrant Mother* next to *Lucretia* but then shifted her near *The Order of Angels*. The Founders Society was planning a fundraising party for opening night, and they wanted to fly an artist in. I couldn't call the artists directly; I had to call their people.

Finally, Bruno ran his eyes over all the pieces again and shook his head. As we walked through the gallery, I wrote down the positions in my pad.

"It's not right." He tapped his foot. "Something...I just don't know."

Bruno folded his arms and wondered.

I walked outside into the bright sun and the air so hot and polluted it ate through me. The steering wheel hurt. I lifted my skirt, draped it over the burning wheel, then made my way home.

The light turned red. Did I push him too far? The light turned green. *What have I done?*

I took a shower and waited on the piece of the porch where the shade hung low. There is no way to see a sun setting over the tilting apartments and not see a world one must accept.

Paul came home.

"I'm sorry," I said.

He kissed me on the cheek. "I'll be down."

He took his shower then returned to find me on the porch with my arms around my knees. He gave me a beer and clinked his to mine. "Congratulate me," he said, "I quit."

The beer tasted icy. I leaned against his shoulder.

"I thought I was indifferent," Paul said. "But you buy into it."

"So are we falling apart or what?"

"What?"

"Your dad said this would last a few months."

Paul shook his head. "I forgot that a long time ago."

He didn't look at me.

"Liar."

He took my hand. "That's all over."

I put my arm around him, and he grabbed me hard. I didn't know what Paul meant. I didn't ask.

Over the next two weeks, Paul drove around a lot. Sometimes we'd drive together and I'd point to buildings with American flags in the windows and Coke bottles with candles and say, "I lived there."

We drove to his old place. It was rotten and boarded up and spray-painted. Grass grew high. Paul said he'd been robbed there so many times he'd lost count. "I moved in with my guitar, my television, and a goldfish. I left with a can of chili."

At home one night I said, "I could ask Bruno. He might know of a job."

"Don't nag me, woman."

"Oh yeah?" I pushed a pillow into his face. "Here's to your computerized sunset."

He grabbed a heavier seat cushion. "Here's to your art farts."

And then we went at it until the dog came up and barked as if to say, "Fun. You're having fun."

I bounced the pillow off the dog's back, and he reached around and bit into it. He pulled in glee, until the cover ripped. Then the dog barked even more, and his tail wagged. He flung the pillow around and then licked the stuffing.

At the end of the two weeks, Paul came home and didn't take a shower, just went inside and grabbed my shoes. My hair was still wet.

"Come on."

We drove past the old recording studio, where Aretha Franklin and the Temptations recorded three decades earlier.

We stopped. The car smelled like sweat and newspapers, and I wanted out. He opened the door. "We're here."

He put his hands over my eyes and walked me to the corner. I didn't trust the ground. I walked with high-lifted steps and thought, *Somewhere there is a curb.*

"You excited?"

"Sure."

He pulled his palms away. "Look."

The one-story, red brick building hid behind a thick crop of weeds and grass. A screen door hung on one hinge, and a ripped, yellow shade drooped in the window. More than one drunk had used the space as a dumping ground for liquor bottles. The fence was peeled back. On one of the prongs, a pair of men's jockey shorts hung like a flag.

"Yeah, and…?"

"It's selling for a dollar."

Something moved in the weeds, and I stepped back.

"Hold out, Paul. You could get it for fifty cents."

His mouth was right next to my ear, his arms around my stomach. "Too late."

He was so happy, happier than I'd seen him in a long time.

"That's great." In that moment, I knew what my mother felt like the day I came home with my hair dyed blue.

Bruno and I worked late the next couple of nights to organize the show. It took four days to find a painter who would fly out and lecture. Bruno settled on an arrangement. It was 7 p.m. when we looked over all the slides. Finally, he grabbed my arm. "We've done it. This is a triumph."

I smiled. It was one of those strange moments that made up for all of Bruno's arrogance. He sat back, pulled a bottle of Scotch from the drawer, and poured us both a drink.

"Our work is complete."

We raised our glasses, but I still wondered about the final piece, Van Gogh's *First Steps*. It seemed too quiet, too gentle. I wanted to end with something bold.

"That is the love that sticks. Let them say what they will."

I smiled, "I agree."

He laughed at my surprise. We swallowed the shots.

I walked outside. Though the air was hot, it had already broken a little. I could smell the mold starting in the leaves.

As I drove away from the museum, I knew Bruno was right. It was art. Though Van Gogh never lived to see the acclaim, that was not the part that mattered.

A driver in a Fairmont passed. His bumper had fallen off. The tailpipe scraped. I pulled up at Paul's little dream and got out of the car. I looked back at the place and my face reflected in the window. It was a face I recognized but, in my heart, did not want to know. It said, "Expect the worst."

I remembered thinking the same thing back in high school. A friend was crying about failing a test. We smoked cigarettes, and I rolled the burning end on the step so the ashes flaked off. "You hoped too much," I said. "Expect the worst. Then you won't be disappointed. Then you won't get hurt."

"You're right," she said.

I don't know where I got such an idea, but I could feel it in the job and in the apartments with the Coke bottle candles. Then I didn't think it was the place at all, just me, just my trip. Maybe I got it from my parents or from their parents, or maybe it was my own invention. But when I looked around, I could see it in the way the view piled up. This tough talk, these safe bets were growing in the weeds, and in the houses, in the McDonald's, and in the buildings left behind. It was in the history, in the junk. The system was rigged against us.

A windowless storage building overshadowed our one-story place like a bully. Not much else on the block had survived. How would we pay the bills and fix this thing? Why did he just up and quit without talking to me first? Three houses across the street slumped in the evening sun. Paul didn't tell me because I would have said no. To restore it, we had to sacrifice our time and risk the debts. I had to see redemption as better than safety. It had been a mom-and-pop place once, a corner store or butcher shop.

Buttercups grew amidst the weeds, and I pulled a few. The moon hung in the daytime sky like a wafer. I walked to the car and glanced back at the building. The windows still looked lonely, and I thought the place needed some lights on or a car parked out front. So I left the car there and walked home. When I glanced back, the place looked comforted, like it belonged.

As I walked past the parking lot of the old recording studio and towards home, I felt an energy rumble through me so hard that I knew something big was going to change. Or maybe it had already. I could see only the road and the crumbling building and those horrible things that stayed the same.

The place Paul bought needed a diner or a gallery. I thought we could pull Jan and Carl into it. They'd sneer at first about it all being beneath them. But after the bitching, they'd pat my back and say, "Cool," and Carl would raise his fist and say, "We're in."

I walked by a newspaper box. Because of work I'd missed everything. There were strikes and fires. Shootings. I looked for the weather, sunny and brisk tomorrow. The date caught my eye: October first.

I ran home. Paul had showered and was sitting on the porch with the dog. The sunset lit him like a fire. The dog barked and ran to me.

As Paul stood up, I thought I hadn't been this happy and lonely in a long time, maybe never. It was Friday night, and we had the whole weekend. Someone else could have the sameness that was out there, down a road, and out past the suburbs, out beyond my wildest belief.

Nothing good was a straight line. What was beautiful knew how to veer on a whim. What I wanted traveled within us and without a name, like a car barreling through the darkness, passing a roadside evangelical travel agent, who proclaimed, "Screw the maps. The America you knew? That land is gone."

# Roby Burns

THE LAST TIME we picked raspberries, my grandfather didn't tell me to pull them gently, or to look for the deep red color, or to notice the way they sagged like hovering bumblebees. As with the seasons before, I had only to look his way and consider how his pale, steady hand coaxed the berries away from their inevitable fall.

He was tall and wore a Scottish cap over his white hair. A black belt secured his blue pants, and under his clothes, he wore pajamas, as did my other grandfather.

We had come to the raspberry field in his big blue car, a two-door, from the factory where he worked. I liked the boxy way of the car and the smell, which was stale but kind. With him, I did not smoke or yell or get mad; I did not slam the door, as I did with my mother. The air was cool. And I had only to sit and watch. My grandfather was quiet, that life-had-happened-to-him stillness. With him, I did not act.

It took some time to drive to the field, but I never had to make small talk. He listened to an AM radio program, the news usually, as we drove along dirt roads where houses sat off in the distance and the fields surrounding them were green and vast.

I did not ask him if it hurt to breathe in coal dust while he worked underground, or what it was like in Terre Haute, or if he saw his brother-in-law die in the mine car accident. He did not ask me what I planned to do with my life, or if I was popular.

We picked in the morning, always the morning, when the berries were ripe and young and possible. When he filled his pail, he peered at my small basketful.

"Good."

When we were done, we walked back to the car. He held the door open for me, and only when I put my seat belt on and the raspberries sat securely on the floor did he close the door softly.

He took me to a fast food restaurant. I didn't know why. Maybe he preferred them, but I thought he might have done it for me, that he guessed it was something I had wanted. I knew not to ask. It would embarrass him. But there was more. He was like the berries. You couldn't pull too much with this question or that question. He was strong. But something in him, something as deep as the mines of his land, seemed perilously cracked. He had lived. And all his living was under safekeeping.

When we got home that day, he stayed for coffee. My mother and grandfather talked of politics and finances and relatives. Sometimes, when he was listening, I saw how his lower lip hung down, how he stared at the floor.

Then, after a moment of concentration, he looked up at me, his granddaughter, and smiled proudly. His pajamas peeped out from under his shirt.

I smiled back. And as soon as he got up to leave, I wished he would stay. I feared something might happen, something new.

After he left, I took a cup, washed the hairy berries and went upstairs with them. I used to put the hollow of the berries on my fingers and pretend they were a pack of fancy ladies. But I was older now and had given up those childish ways.

Instead, I ate one dewy berry and tasted it and everything there—the earth, the sun, the water, and something else, something that took a long time, something that could not be named but was good and true and long lasting. In tasting this, a seed had been planted, a gift bequeathed, so it was not all too late.

The moment spoke to something bigger than the Depression or destitution or my anger. Parents, two generations ago, had made sure the message was hidden, tucked in the sun and earth of their child where storms and winters were sure to come.

I thought neither of accidents, nor trouble. No, I thought of his name, and of the pajamas peeping out from under his shirt, and how all things turn to a sort of sleep that prepares them for morning, and how all parts of this world, from the coal mines to the burdened limbs, must know the weight of their time.

# The Family Trip

MY SISTER MEGHAN didn't have much of a choice when the three pretty girls surrounded her. They were black and white, short and tall, and infamous at the school for their unified gaits, laughing as they walked, with their graceful gestures and sharp elbows. To see them together was like watching flamingos in a moving watercolor, padding their way home through the neighborhood of drooping brick houses with bad roofs and rusting cars. If their singular motions didn't stop people cold, their lilting, insincere comments ("Nice sweater" and "You cut your hair") did. Their cruelty felt like a knife slicing wide, revealing nothing at first, then relentless blood pouring at once.

The girls didn't notice Meghan until the school's junior high art show, where work was propped up on easels or folding tables. The fourth-to-sixth graders missed class to tour the display. The fourth graders wanted to touch the slumping clay mugs. Some swiped their fingers along the pencil drawings of animals and family members. The teachers had to pull away their sweaty hands, which stopped the procession cold. Some sixth-grade boys shoved one another and hollered like they were at a basketball game. I looked for Meghan's work, and saw it, a painting that resembled our garage, with our beat-up car parked in front. I was embarrassed, until I saw the blue ribbon that said "First Prize."

"Wow," I said.

My best friend, Janice, peered in and pointed. "Hey, that's your house!"

When the school day ended, I wanted to run home through the leaves to tell Mom first. But Meghan walked ahead of me, dragging her black art case, surrounded by the pretty girls. I hung back as they laughed. They were always giggling and laughing. What was so damned funny? Meghan looked so much shorter with them, more awkward. They left Meghan at our house, then smiled and waved back before they moved on together.

Meghan wasn't thin, and we couldn't afford nice clothes. More than this, the girls' watercolor souls were sure to bleed at the first spilled drink or blob of rain. Meghan was oil paint on canvas—sturdy, thick, committed. I wasn't like art at all. I was like the dogs, with keen senses, who smelled danger and barked at things otherwise unseen. I could sniff out trouble on winding paths. After graduation from junior high, they would never call Meghan again, or worse, they would go to the same high school and ignore her, or worse still, make fun of her. They had already gone in droves, or people like them—Cadillac families with money, broom-handle posture, and ambitions—to Birmingham, Royal Oak, some as far as Ann Arbor. White flight. My mother said they destroyed the tax base, which just meant there was no money to fix anything. So the roads crumbled, the renters moved in, and crime rose. We didn't know what was happening, because we were in the eye of it, feeling the sky churn around us.

The day after the walk, Meghan went on a diet. She'd gone on diets before, but this time she restricted herself to 1,000 calories. It took a few days to memorize the calorie counts and deal with Mom's protests. Meghan and I shared the same room. On the third night, stretched out in her double bed, she ticked off the calorie count of lettuce, carrots, oatmeal, and tomatoes. Chip, our dog, curled up at the end of my bed, groaning at her conversation.

In school that day, we'd learned about full moons and how each one had a name honoring a plant or animal. I stared at the ceiling with the gauzy window reflection cast there by April's hare moon, listening to Meghan review her food intake as though recounting defense strategies in war. Today she was victorious. "I ate a potato without butter for dinner, a slice of roast half the size of my fist, and broccoli."

"Sounds boring," I said.

"I didn't drink pop at all. You know, that's the first time in, like, a year."

I rolled over on my side. Chip got up, circled three times, and sat back down in a humph. When Meghan talked about her skin and weight, Chip lifted up his head.

His ears perked in curiosity. "Chip wants to sleep," I said.

"Oh, shut up. Tomorrow I'll have oatmeal for breakfast with two tablespoons of milk and some fruit."

"You shut up." Chip stretched out, then flipped over onto his back. Then he started swinging his body from side to side. "Hey, stop. You'll fall."

Chip didn't care. He twisted one way then another, his tongue out, making funny panting noises. Then he sprang up to attention, wagged his tail, and barked. I petted his head and laughed.

"Hush." I shook my finger at him. He licked it.

"You should go on a diet, too," Meghan said.

She thought I was fat.

"You know what'll help you sleep?" I asked.

"What?"

"Ice cream."

Chip licked my hand.

"I can't," she said, with a determined tone, as though her deprivation was a sculpting knife. It bugged Mom senseless.

Mom cooked our oatmeal, our eggs, our bacon on the weekends. She roasted our meats and flavored our stews with tips from Julia Child and skills she picked up while working at a restaurant. But her skills were always tested by two impediments. The first was our big family: five, including Rob, my brother, who was 6'3" and on the basketball team, so he ate like two people. Mom took Meghan's diet in stages—personal offense, then annoyance, then guilt. The next night at dinner, Mom said, "It's not like we can always afford roast, why can't you just eat a piece of it?"

Money was the second impediment. The days after payday Mom cooked in her glory, her face peering over steaming pots of potato, or pasta for our chicken, our flank steak. We had to eat our greens. After the first week we ate less chicken and more potatoes. No crackers, no cheese, no snacks. At a week and a half, Mom cooked oatmeal for breakfast, canned tuna and peas for dinner.

Meghan remained resolute, indifferent to the patterns ahead. She'd reached her 1,000-calorie limit, so she chewed only raw carrots at the table. "I have to stay on this calorie count for a month."

"A month?" Mom yelled. "You'll be dead by then."

"I'll eat hers," Rob said.

Meghan was only fourteen, Mom said. So legally she had no right to starve herself.

"You want me to be fat," Meghan said.

"You're not fat," Mom said. Mom used to be chubby, too. Her brothers teased her, so Mom decided to eat half of everything on her plate. Then she lost weight.

"I tried that. I gained a pound."

I was curious. "So at eighteen, can she starve herself, you know, legally?"

"Shut up, Mary," Meghan said.

"You shut up," I said.

"Both of you pipe down," Dad said. "Eat, already. People are starving out there."

Rob nodded. "The famine in Ethiopia. We had a fundraiser at school."

"I mean around here," Dad said. He made a circular motion with his knife. "Within a mile, people are sitting down to nothing."

"It's my fault," Mom said. She didn't elaborate.

I could have told Mom not to worry. True, Meghan walked home with her new friends, and went to a birthday party, but in a few days the girls would grow bored, and Meghan would eat again. My confidence waned, though, on the following Paycheck Thursday. Dad came home with loads of groceries. We sifted through vegetables and meats, the apples and the crackers, to salvage the potato chips, dip, and pop. We divided the chips evenly into three bowls, but Meghan said, "I don't want them," with her chin in the air. She helped Mom put groceries away.

"Good," Rob said, and poured her lot into his.

"I get some," I said. But he was already in the TV room, spread out on the shag carpeting, scooping up the dip with his chips and shoveling them into his mouth.

Meghan sat with us, but this time on the edge of the couch, as if posing. We watched *Kojak* and *Good Times*. She drank lemon water while Chip licked dip off Rob's paper plate. Rob said, "Good boy."

"I don't even want it anymore," she said, proud of herself. "It smells gross."

"Good," Rob said. "More for me."

A Little Caesar's Pizza commercial came on and Meghan shifted on the couch. Rob turned to Meghan and said, "So do you have to give up pizza, like, forever?"

"You're pigs," Meghan said. She stood up and left.

Because Meghan wouldn't eat much, she spent most nights staring at the ceiling. One night she turned on the radio. Songs like "Goodbye Yellow Brick Road" and "All By Myself" played. I liked the songs before 11:00 p.m., but by midnight, the music kept me awake. I got up to turn it off, but when I did Meghan said, "Leave it on, jerk."

"I can't sleep," I said.

"Now you know how it feels."

"I hate your friends," I said.

And then she said it. "Well I hate you."

"Like I care," I said. But inside, my heart broke. I stayed up all night and watched the dawn. I hated the rip in my covers. I hated people, my school, and my old clothes. I just wanted her to like me. Why was that so hard?

Once my sister and I did everything together. When she went to work at the mall, Dad would drop us both off and I would run around, look at jewelry, and read in the bookstore. She took me to see *Jaws*. We had to stand in a long line. Inside the theatre, only single seats remained, so we sat together in the aisle. I screamed, but so did everybody.

A woman near us asked, "Is that girl old enough to be here?"

"Her?" Meghan asked. "She's 16."

The woman shook her head. "If she's 16, I'm Gladys Knight."

I leaned over. "You look like Gladys Knight." The woman smiled, then people told us to shut up. I kept screaming.

After the movie, Meghan showed me her arm with the fresh wounds from where my nails had dug in.


The morning after Meghan proclaimed her hate, she said, "Time to get serious and exercise."

"Okay, what are we doing?"

"Running."

"Running?"

"Yeah, two miles."

I couldn't find Chip's leash, so I used a rope. He jumped on me and scraped my arm while I tied it to his collar. On our first run, Chip took off like we were racing for our lives. Our neighbor, Mr. Watson, nodded once, but inside I wondered if he wasn't thinking, *There go those crazy white girls.* I had to breathe hard as we passed the neighbors, the people we didn't know, then an older guy who shook his head at us. Did we look so awful? My head started to tingle. "Too fast," I said and sat down on the lawn. Chip came back and licked my face. He was our only happy runner, with an expression like, *Isn't this the best thing ever.*

Meghan ran half a block ahead before she saw me and jogged back. "Running is the key. We'll be thin in no time."

We started again. Meghan slowed down to keep pace with me, but I still lagged behind, huffing. I stopped again and tipped my head over. Chip's tongue hung out the side of his mouth. No matter how much I inhaled, it wasn't enough. Meghan said, "You have to be strong. We can do this."

I nodded. And we were running again. We made it to 7 Mile, blocks short of our goal. And when we got home we ate oatmeal with wheat germ.

We ran several more times together. One morning I thought I would faint from hunger. We still didn't make it to two miles, but we were close. I was proud of myself. I could keep up with Meghan.

After two weeks, though, Meghan was frustrated. "I lost two pounds."

"That's good."

"How much did you lose?"

"Seven."

She blocked her face with a magazine.

"What're you reading?"

"*Glamour.*"

I plopped on my bed. "That sounds stupid."

"Whatever."

The next day Mom made Dad a plate of eggs and hash browns. Dad asked if Meghan wanted some. She said no. Dad got up to get juice. She ate one bite, then a forkful. By the end, she scraped the last bite up with a spoon. We stopped running.


Meghan got the idea of a liquid protein diet from a *Glamour* article. She started it the day after the breakfast incident.

Meghan hung out more with her snotty friends. The money she saved for art supplies Meghan now spent on new shirts and jewelry. They still walked together, with Meghan in the middle. Their constant giggling felt weird in a neighborhood that mixed a Black Power vibe with the Business Dad thing. It was funny watching muscle-bound guys from the Powerhouse Gym walk by dads with paunches. I saw this one dad sniff and huff, as if he'd just been accused of something. This gargantuan dude nodded, and smiled, but was too busy admiring his own lumpy arms and small waist to notice anyone else.

In a week, Meghan lost weight. She told me I needed to pick up my side of the room.

Worse than any of this was the music that played all night.

I would turn it off. Meghan would throw a fit. Chip barked, sensing my anger.

We fought. Mom had read someone called Spock, who was not on *Star Trek*, and he said to let kids work it out. But after more days of yelling and starvation, Mom saw a priest.

Meghan and I barely spoke. When school ended, our mother said to get ready for "our trip."

"What trip?" Meghan asked.

"Our vacation," Mom said. She folded laundry, not looking at us. "The one we've been planning for two months."

Meghan eyed Mom with suspicion. "You never told us this."

I didn't want to go on a trip with Meghan. She was mean. Plus, we'd have to leave Chip in the care of our neighbors. "I'll sit this one out," I said, all nonchalant. "Don't worry about us. Chip and I, we'll stay here together, guard the house."

Mom raised her eyebrow. "You're going. The dog stays."

"Spock would take Chip."

Rob walked by. "Spock doesn't own a dog, doof. He's in space."

I glared at Mom, waiting for her to correct Rob. She never did.

"This is futile," I said. I'd just learned the word in school. I glanced at Mom to assess my usage.

She smiled. "Go pack."

Meghan said she would run out of liquid protein shakes. My mom said they would stop and get more.

"Do you promise?" Meghan asked. She studied Mom like her movements were drawings.

Mom stopped folding her clothes. "Why would I lie?"

I told Chip the entire plan. While we were gone, Janice and her family would look after him. And then we would be back in two weeks. I pointed to the date on the calendar. He licked his bone, pretending not to be crushed.

The day we left, I vowed to hate the trip, partly out of allegiance to Chip. But there were other issues. When you have an older brother and sister, for example, you have to be careful how you sit in the middle of the back seat, because if you lean over and, God forbid, touch one of them, they get pissed off and shove you into the other sibling, which pisses her off and then you are pushed back and forth like a pinball in a machine. Then you know this vacation will be hell for you, and a fun game for everyone else.

It wasn't just me. Janice was the youngest and she said the older ones call her the "baby" with a judgmental scowl, like she orchestrated the birthing line. Everything she said was on a sliding scale from stupid to stupidest. They rolled their eyes, which was like verbal shoving. It still hurt.

"Mom and Dad won't make it stop, either," she said. "They're like, 'oh, they don't really mean it.'"

I nodded in commiseration.

My brother was cool and I was a moron. My sister was artistic and I was still a moron. I put my knees together, lifted my shoulders, and braced for balance.

We stopped to eat at the Sherwood Forest Diner. We sat in a booth and I got to sit next to Mom. Meghan drank ice water. I missed Chip so much. I took a bite of my food, vowed to leave the rest as a protest. Mom asked if I liked my waffle.

I sighed. "It's okay."

"Well you ate the whole thing."

I whispered to Mom, "I miss Chip."

"We just left him," Mom said.

"He's probably tearing the trash apart," I said. Chip did this when we left him at home.

"We took the trash out," she said.

"He'll chew the cushions. He hates to be left behind."

"I put them in my room."

Rob leaned in, "What're you talking about? Chip?"

I whispered to Mom, "Can't we bring him with us? He'll be good, I promise." Janice's family would take good care of Chip. They would keep him in the house at first and feed him twice a day, and they promised me to let him out four times a day. But still, he might die of loneliness.

"Where would we put him?" Meghan asked.

"With the luggage in the back."

"No," Mom said. "He has to watch the house."

My brother shoved a pile of cut-up pancake into his mouth. "You're such a moron."

She was right. People had tried to break in a few times. One time, Chip was locked in our room, and my father used this rumbling shout that sounded like a bear. Chip barked at the door until Meghan opened it and he sprang downstairs as the criminal fled the scene.

Mom said, "Meghan, will you miss your new friends?"

"They said they would write letters while I was gone, so I would see them in the mailbox when I got back."

"Oh, that's nice," Mom said. I rolled my eyes. How stupid. I didn't expect Janice to write, and we were real friends.

When we left the diner, a pink haze hovered over the droopy storefronts. People in old clothes walked the streets, as if their job was wandering the earth. It was Saturday, and Livernois was dead, with wrappers in the curbsides and tufts of weeds breaking through cracks in the sidewalks.

I looked back once, and saw the landscape and thought of Chip. In two weeks nothing bad would happen. He would guard the house, and mope, and wait for our return. When we did, he would jump on me with glee.

I sat with my knees together, reading a book, trying to be good, because if I was good people would like me. When we took a left, I tipped toward Meghan. I said, "Sorry," but she shoved me into my brother, who shoved me, too. It went back and forth like that.

On the road we fell into our routines. Meghan sketched with a pencil, Rob looked at baseball cards and slept. I read *Travels with Charley*. I loved the dream worlds best, so I started to feel good after twenty pages, then fifty, then one hundred. My book was about Steinbeck traveling with his dog. When I was old, Chip and I would travel together, just like that.

We saw the yellow Stuckey's sign and Rob grabbed the seatback and leaned forward: "Dad, look. A Stuckey's. Come on."

Meghan said, "Stuckey's?"

It was our favorite place from the last trip.

Dad glanced at Mom, who said, "I'm hungry."

Dad turned the blinker on, and looked to the right and left before pulling off. Meghan had always loved Stuckey's. It was more serene than other fast food restaurants. The one we drove to was set in a backdrop of rolling hills and farms. It sat alone amidst the green, like a dream.

We ordered chicken, fries, and coleslaw. Still, Meghan wouldn't eat. When she ordered a Tab, we thought that was different. Dad ordered two meals for himself, because he had to think more than us. She poured the liquid protein into the Tab, which made it fizz and go flat.

"Yuck," she said.

"I'll get you a water," Dad said. "That looks terrible."

While he was gone, Mom said, "Meghan, we'll get you water for the car ride, but have one fry at least, until you can get your nourishment. Here."

Mom slid the plate over. "Take it from your father's extra."

I sat next to Mom, my fingers slick from the chicken. Meghan blinked, her eyes wide from hunger. Her skin was pale, her lips dry. Dad stood in the long line.

"He won't mind," Mom said. So Meghan took one, and bit into it carefully, like it could hurt her. She chewed.

Rob said, "Can I have Dad's extra chicken?"

Meghan slid the plate closer. "No."

When Dad came back, he glanced at the half-empty plate.

"Sorry, Dad," Meghan said.

He put his hand on Mom's shoulder. "If you're happy, I'm happy."

Meghan smiled, and ate the rest.

Mom gave me a napkin, but I licked the grease off my fingers.

Rob said, "I'd be happy with more chicken."

Mom said, "We all get one plate."

Rob shook his head. "What a rip."

On the ride out, I said, "That was so good."

"That was the best chicken I've ever tasted," Meghan said, and she sat back.

My head nodded for a bit, and when I woke up, we were driving through a forest. Meghan slept, her head resting on the crease between the seat and the door.

I leaned forward and tapped Mom on the shoulder. "Where are we?"

"Close to the Smokies," she said. Meghan woke up.

When we neared the Smoky Mountains, Meghan said, "Look."

"What?"

I leaned over, and said, "I can't see anything."

"No, put your head out the window." When I did, I could see fog resting on top of mountains so mighty they reminded me of breathing, living things, like slumbering bears. They rose so high they disappeared into clouds. My mother looked back at us.

"Isn't it lovely?" she asked.

The trees became so tall I couldn't see their tops. The dirt was black, and the woods were huge, majestic, and plentiful. Soon we drove through a canopy of green, our faces pressed against the glass, and saw a group of beasts, resembling hairy pigs, run between the trees.

Dad slowed down and glanced over. "They're boar. Those are wild boar."

The boar ran away with their little high-heeled feet.

"Those were the first boar I've ever seen," my father said.

"Yes," Mom said. Even the back of her head smiled.

We climbed up the mountain, on roads thin and perilous. The sides were craggy with rocks, trees, and shrubs. The motor chugged as we kept going. And when we were about halfway up, we drove in fog, the moist air on our faces.

You had to veer right to stay on the path. It sloped up forever. The fog was thick, and the ground damp. A white car drove in front of us. And then, as Dad recounted later, the car's left turn signal blinked. Dad thought that was weird. It must have been a mistake. Nothing to worry about. The driver sped up a little, then slowed down, looked to the left, and turned the car left, as if moving into a parking spot. That's how Dad described it later. I looked out the window at the fog when I saw the car gently tip over the mountain. I saw something fly out of the car. Its back end lifted on the descent, like a duck's behind when diving into water for food. And then the car disappeared.

There was no crash. I figured it was a steep side road.

Rob hoisted himself up. "Cool, that guy just drove off the cliff."

Dad slowed down, then stopped on the right side of the road. Cars passed us. We heard the crash then. But we didn't feel the ground move. The mountain absorbed the impact of clashing metal. We all looked over, and there sat the driver, his open palms bracing against the ground, his butt and feet planted. He stared at the distance. Dad watched, waiting for something to happen, then Mom whispered to Dad, and he moved back on the road.

"He jumped out," Meghan said. "We should help the guy."

"He's okay," Dad said.

"That was weird," Meghan said.

"Why did the car go over?" I asked.

Dad looked at me in the rearview mirror and glanced at Mom. "He lost control."

Mom nodded. But it didn't feel right. The guy wanted to kill himself, and one slim thought stopped him. We grew very quiet in the car, except for Rob.

"It's like Evel Knievel, but live," Rob said.

Meghan touched my arm and said, "It's all right. He changed his mind."

I looked up to her. She smiled at me in a way I'd never seen before. "He didn't want to do it."

I blinked tears she must have thought were for the man. She put her hand on my shoulder. I felt like the most important person ever.

"You're right," I said.

We went other places, strange places, flatlands and small towns. Rigs like metal pelicans slurping oil from bone-dry Texas flatlands.

In a place that sounded like Armadillo, we stopped at Cadillac Ranch, where ten Cadillacs had been half buried, snouts first, into the ground, tilting westward.

Dad said the Cadillacs were slanted at the same angle as the pyramids. They were old cars, with different back ends and shapes.

"So what's the point?" Rob said.

Dad shrugged. "I think it's supposed to be about us."

"Us?" Mom asked. She squinted her eyes.

Meghan said, "The death of the auto companies, you know, Detroit."

Dad sighed.

"That's dumb," Rob said.

A few days later, we headed south through dry, flat roads. Dad said, "This is Mexico," and two guys on the side of the road sang "We're an American Band" but changed the words to "We're a Mexican Band." It was dusty. We went to dinner someplace good. Meghan said, "It's beautiful." She took more Polaroids. At the hotel she studied them, then wrote cards to the pretty girls. When she was done with the cards, she looked them over, tilted her head at the cursive, then applied the stamps. We left the next day.

In New Mexico, we opened the windows all the way down. My hair whipped around and smacked me in the face. Mom said, "What is that?" Meghan poked her head out the window, alarmed at something ahead. "No. No way. Stop the car."

"What?" Rob asked.

He put his head way out. "Oh, shit."

Mom shook her finger. "No swearing."

"Stop," they both yelled. Dad kept driving.

Then Dad stopped. I didn't see what was happening until the shadow came from above. I leaned over Meghan and put my head out of the car. A large boulder, impossibly big, hovered over the road, above us. It had no way of staying in position. It defied gravity, should be falling, and felt more troubling for its suspension.

"Imagine that," Dad said, sticking his head out the window. "Do you think this is safe?"

My mother laughed. My brother and sister screamed and shoved my father's shoulder, pushed at the seatback. "Go, hurry up. We're gonna die!"

As we pulled away, we looked back. The hanging boulder didn't make sense. It was framed by the auburn-red hills of New Mexico, getting smaller, then inconsequential, then dreamlike in the pattern of the horizon.

We stopped at a corner store so Meghan could mail the postcards to the pretty girls.

All the days bled together then, under the sun, and within the bowls of red dirt, and then the flatlands of Iowa, with hair-parted cornfields.

We didn't stop much on the way home, not until Indiana. Mom and Dad wanted to go to dinner, so they left us at the hotel. The sky darkened toward night. We watched TV and ate Big Macs when the news came on. A tornado had touched down. Rob said, "Cool." When we looked out the window, we realized the darkness was from gathering clouds. I stood by the window.

"When are they coming back?" I asked.

Meghan said, "Soon. Don't worry."

I started to tear up, but I wouldn't sniffle, otherwise Rob and Meghan would call me a moron. But what if they didn't come back, and then we would never get home, and Chip would wonder and worry. Rob stretched out on the other bed. Meghan came over and sat next to me. "It's gonna be all right. You'll see."

I wiped my tears away. "Don't be mean."

She put her arm around me. "I won't be mean. I'll sit here with you. We'll watch them pull into the parking lot. They'll park right where they did the last time, right there."

"Where?"

"See?" she asked, second spot from the lawn. "Dad always parks in the same spot."

Rob thought about it and laughed. "That's true." He went back to watching television.

I woke up in the night, and everyone was in the room, with the two beds and the cot, and the lights off. Meghan was by my side.

I poked Meghan. "What happened?"

"They came back," she said and rolled over.

I couldn't wait to see Chip. I would hear him bark before anyone opened the door. I'd hoped he'd ripped things, shredded blankets or coats or shoes in anger, so my parents would never leave him again. Was he angry at being abandoned or did he see our departure as reckless? How would we ever survive without him? Either way, when we returned, Chip always looked a bit ashamed of his outbursts, his tail wagging slightly, as if he hoped we wouldn't notice.

As we passed the corner gas station and drove through 6 Mile Road, the hazy, leaden sky cast a pall over the houses. When we pulled up to our block, I felt as though we'd been in orbit and finally landed at our house of red brick and yellow lawn, cement porch, and storm door with the ripped screen.

The Johnsons walked outside when we pulled up. Mr. and Mrs. Johnson were kind, durable people who'd suffered so harshly through the Depression they maintained a chest freezer full of food, so they would never again endure that aching hunger. They wore clothes in the same fashion as my parents: fathers in plaid, short-sleeved shirts, mothers in pullover tops with slacks and sneakers.

Mr. Johnson looked worried and shuffled his feet as my dad got out. "Hello, Bill. How'd it go?"

When Mom opened the door, Chip ran out, jumping and barking until he tipped me over and started licking my face. "I told you we'd be back." I grabbed his collar, and we followed the others inside.

How different the house looked: the walls dull, the rugs worn to the threads at the corners. The lamps. The pictures of Jesus.

"Welcome home," Mr. Johnson said. Janice talked to me about the summer fun I'd missed and the people who moved away.

I went upstairs to check my room and found my clothes were strewn across the carpeting; a circle of dog hair collected on my ripped cover, where Chip slept while we were gone.

I closed my eyes and kissed Chip on the top of his head, then he followed me downstairs.

The Johnsons said they were worried sometimes when they could hear Chip barking. But no one had broken in.

"When we first came in, Chip growled. I thought he might bite us."

My dad threw his hand out. "That dog, you toss a piece of pizza at him, and he's your friend for life."

Chip perked his ears and looked up at me. It wasn't true. Chip had bitten so many dogs and people that we had to hide him upstairs and hold his mouth closed when Animal Control came by. My mom told the men that we didn't own a dog.

Chip gave the Johnsons a pass, but they weren't his pack. One false move and they would have gotten it, too.

Now Chip returned to his happy panting. He barked once.

Meghan sifted through the mail, pretending to be indifferent. Of course there were no letters from her new friends. Chip leaned into me. Soon the Johnsons left. We hadn't bought them anything. That is what I wished now, that we had bought them something as a thank you.

Mom went to the kitchen to "assess the food situation." The rest of us hauled in the suitcases, beach hats, spare sandals, dirty tennis shoes, and books from the car. With the last suitcase inside and the door closed, Dad asked, "Who wants pizza?"

"Me!" my brother and sister replied. "Pepperoni! Cheese! Get two!"

I went back upstairs and stretched out on the bed. Finally, I had some room. Chip put his chin on the bed, and I patted the mattress twice, which in dog language meant, *Come on up.* He crept up carefully, trying to be good. He sat in a circle and licked my leg. I thought he would lie still, but happiness and relief over my return overwhelmed him, and he pawed at my hand to pet him more.

"You're right," I said. "It's not safe without you."

If I stopped petting him, Chip would nudge my hand to keep going. I could see in his eyes a knowing, a message. I dreaded the days to come, the yelling, the radio, Meghan going back to face the ridicule of the watercolor girls. I wished we could be on the road forever.

In those weeks the radio played, Chip rested his chin on my hand, which was dog language for *Be calm and wait.* So I let the radio go. I never complained. When school started again, the pretty girls walked with Meghan, but I could tell, even from a distance, it wasn't the same. Meghan smiled tightly, her eyes wide, as if seeking approval for something. They sensed it. I imagined they saw her weight gain, or just got bored. Then one day I saw Meghan lug her wide art case. She was alone, but held her head high, as if nothing had ever happened. She'd gotten away without much pain, just rejection, which was all right.

They walked together one more time. It was a warm fall day. The girls cut through the parking lot, and north on Belden. Meghan headed east down Santa Maria toward home, so they met where the streets crossed. The girls talked in a high pitch and with elaborate hand gestures. Meghan's head stayed focused. They nodded and glanced at one another. At our house, Meghan put one hand up to say goodbye and walked up to the house without looking back. One of the girls put her hand to her heart, as if something were sad. I was so proud of Meghan. They could do or say anything. But Meghan didn't give an inch. Kind, but distant. Aloof, but respectful.

That same night, Mom asked Meghan if she wanted to invite the girls over for dinner. I took my fork to the green beans and steered them around my plate.

"Maybe some other time," she said. "My art teacher wants me to work on a piece for Friday."

Later, in our room, Meghan walked in and said, "I'm tired." She walked to the clock radio to turn it on.

Chip was squirreling on his back again, doing his happy dance.

Meghan pushed the buttons on the radio.

"Hey," she said. She looked at it. It didn't work at all.

"You broke it," she said.

"Plug it in, doof."

"Oh."

She plugged it in. It still didn't work.

"What the hell?"

"Try another plug."

She did. Chip twisted and turned on his back.

"You broke it, didn't you?"

"You broke it," I said. "Overuse. Just tell Dad. He'll get it fixed."

"Cut it out," I said to Chip, then laughed. He would give it all away. Chip smiled, his tongue sticking out.

He growled, in a funny way.

It was his idea in the first place. Earlier that day, he watched me, of course, take apart the radio and gut it, as if it were a rabbit or a squirrel. The actions were so familiar, Chip sniffed, as though there might be something delicious hidden in there, some purpose to this noisy beast.

Now I said to Meghan, "Let's get Dad to take us to the art store this weekend."

She sat down on the bed. "Good idea. You sure you didn't break it?"

"I didn't break your stupid radio."

Chip kept writhing and twisting, his tongue hanging out, with a thrill that almost made him fall off the bed. He barked once, as if he couldn't stand to hold it in anymore. He flipped upright, dizzy with glee that his pack hadn't abandoned him. He barked again.

"Chip," Meghan said. "Calm down." His wet, bulbous nose touched my arm as he sniffed, then he huffed in a way I once saw as joy, but now knew had been a message all along.

*Watch how a pro does this*, he said. *Love, but never obey.*

# The Patron Saint
# of Lost Girls

IT WAS 1976. A reporter said her body had been neatly placed near a mound by the freeway, in clear view of the Troy Police Department. We watched it on our black-and-white television. It was two days after Christmas and I couldn't stop staring at a large gray blob on the snowbank.

"Police will not say if this murder is linked to a previous killing. Worried parents want to know: could this be the work of a serial killer? Is there an Oakland County Killer?"

"Why does the killer get a title?" Meghan said, pissed off, because she was always pissed off. I was surprised she didn't yell at me for sitting on her bed to watch the news story. We shared a room for ten years, and she never let me sit on the bed. This time, she sat down next to me.

"What's that spot?" I asked.

"Where?"

"In the snow, see?"

She leaned forward to the small black-and-white television.

"Is it blood?" I asked. The tears welled up in my eyes. I didn't want to cry in front of Meghan. She'd call me a baby if I cried.

The reporter showed a picture of Jill again.

"He's not nobility," Meghan said. "They should call him Ugly Stupid Farting Man."

"I know her," I said. Meghan went quiet.

Jill and I went to grade school together. She left before sixth grade. No one knew why.

"She was nice," I said.

"They're always nice."

My sister's friend had been raped and murdered the year before, while babysitting. Jill and the babysitter lived in suburbia, which was supposed to be safer than where we lived.

"It must be blood," I said.

Meghan put her arm around me, then nudged me. "It could be anything."

"They would say if it was blood, right?"

"The kid should get a title."

"Like what? Oakland County Victim?" I asked.

"No, doof. Like, Jill Robinson, the Martyr of Royal Oak."

I didn't like the word martyr. It was like victim. "What about Jill, Patron Saint of Lost Girls."

"That's good," she said. "Not bad for a moron."

"Thanks, asshole."

She took her arm away, as if the moment should end. But neither of us wanted to get up.

So we sat, shoulder-to-shoulder, huddled together while another young victim's face flashed on the screen.

We hurried to ordain him.

"Mark Stebbins, Patron Saint of Ferndale," Meghan said.

I nodded in approval.

"When they find the killer, he'll be just a pervert with a name," my sister said. "You'll see."

Over the next few weeks we tried to remember. We really did. I wrote their names and titles down, taped them to a wall.

Two more victims were found that winter. Each time, Meghan and I huddled in front of the television to bequeath titles, to anoint them for posterity.

"Kristine Mihelich, Protector of Ten-Year-Olds," I said.

"Tim King, Saint of Skateboarders."

We sat on Meghan's bed, our mouths open.

"They'll never find him," I said.

Meghan gripped my arm. "They will. You'll see."

I thought of the unsuspecting kids, clutching candy or backpacks, getting on bikes, or walking toward home, then suddenly, gone from the picture, erased, sucked through time.

I added Kristine and Tim's names and titles to the list. Every day, I'd check the newspaper for more kids. Every day, Meghan and I would add them to our prayers. The families of the victims went on the news, pleading for people to come forward. In the ensuing weeks, I applied fresh tape to my list on the wall. Police said they were following leads. Months later, when Meghan and I were fighting, I looked to the wall and stopped cold.

"Shut up," I said. "Look."

"What?"

Something in my face must have freaked her out, because she turned slowly, carefully.

Meghan put her hand to her heart.

Like the saints of our youth, even the list had vanished.

# The Driving Lesson

THE DAY AFTER my father banned me from the car for the rest of my life, we were back on the road. What else could he do? When faced with the will of a teenage girl, a man's strength collapses like outhouse walls in a tornado. My father sat beside me and buckled his seatbelt with more drama than was necessary. He sighed gravely.

"It was one red light," I said.

He turned and stared at me. A dumb stare. "Red lights... grenades, suicides. One's all it takes."

"I fail to see the connection."

A kid flew by on a banana-seat bike.

"You should sit here."

"That's not very supportive." I looked at myself in the rearview mirror and smoothed my bangs over what I considered to be my disgustingly long forehead. My father believed that this fixation would kill him.

"Why don't I call the EMS and they can follow us to the accident?"

"I'm going to tell Mom."

He fell quiet and sank in his seat. We were good at these tasteful threats, like mobsters. But then, we deserved it. My father and I were the angry ones of the family, lured into embarrassing dramas and sulking fits that my mother, brother, and sister had learned to walk around as though we were potted plants that tended to heave themselves from the windowsill.

Meghan would have agreed, but she had moved downtown to a studio apartment to paint. My brother complained about sharing a car with three other drivers. My mother seemed amused by the complaints, because her power never required such trivial actions. She had a righteous indignation that was pure and mighty and spellbound. She prayed, not like she was giving thanks, but as though she were walking down a long, dark hallway to lodge a complaint at the home office.

One day she got angry with the neighbor for breaking the fence in a drunken touch football game. "You call that a fence?" the neighbor said. "That's white-trash chicken wire."

My father and I said someone should take a stand; one of us should throw the glove down. We paced around the house, burning oil, until the next day when our neighbor keeled over and died. Heart attack, my father said, and we both glanced at my mother.

"Oh, dear." She put her thin fingers to her mouth.

"Can we get you anything, Theresa?" my father asked. "Have a seat. I'll make dinner."

"You're not mad at us or anything, are you, Mom?" my brother asked.

My father was the calm and the storm. At dinner, his pensiveness reminded me of all the unsaid things in the world. The table had led many lives. The peas had made long journeys. And anger percolated years before it ever burst into action. After my first driving lesson, my father refused to take his hands off his head and walked around the house until he saw my mother and yelled, "You were nearly a widow!" I shot back, "Oh...you've never made any mistakes?"

I ran up the stairs and slammed the door. That's when my father yelled, "No car, no car. Banned for life!"

To which my mother replied, "She's *your* daughter."

But a scant forty minutes later, we smelled Canadian bacon and humbly made our way to the dinner table.

"I see the trauma hasn't affected your appetites," my mother said, as we sheepishly passed the potatoes. Reasonably jovial spirits returned.

"I remember my first driving lesson with your grandfather," Mom said.

"Yeah?"

"I hit a tree."

We all laughed, not because it was so funny but from the sweetness of remembering my grandfather, dead six years and, at the time, a helpless passenger barreling toward a worried oak.

"What did he say?"

"'How many more kids do I have, after you?' I sat there looking at the crumpled metal and the bark and said, 'Ten.' And he said, 'Jesus above.' Then he pulled out a bill and said, 'Here's a tenner—a buck for each kid. Tell them all I'll be right home. Give me a running start, an hour at least, to get out of town.'"

"What'd you do?" I asked.

"I ran home and told everyone. When your grandfather came home two hours later smelling of smoke, all the kids ran around him and said, 'You're back, you're back,' and he said, 'Where else would I know to go?'"

We sat and let the spoons slide into the ice cream.

"So, it's settled," I said. "Tomorrow, we are on the road again."

My father reached into the box of ice cream again. My mother raised her eyebrow. "A man deserves a last meal," he said.

"Honestly," she replied.

The next day I stopped decidedly at every stop sign. Leaves fell like little parachutes, and the trees modeled their red and orange hairdos. My father did not do much to smooth out the mood. "Look out! Car. Pull over. Car!"

He was missing the Lions game. It was Sunday afternoon, and parked cars lined both sides of the road. My mother insisted we drive during the game, when the most troublesome drivers were inside "smashing beer cans against their foreheads." My father believed he would be home by halftime.

"Car!" He pressed his foot to the floor.

Our car was large and boxy and bounced on its shocks like a catamaran. I veered into a gap between the parked cars, and the rear end stuck out into the road. The driver behind me had to steer to the left and then to the right to get around me. A small woman peered over her wheel and shook her fist at me. The dogs in the Rogers' yard stood on their hind legs and watched us like gossipy neighbors.

As I steered back into traffic, I hit the bumper of a parked LeBaron. "You're making me nervous," I said.

"I'm making you nervous? Slow down," he said. "Where's the fire?"

He was my father, and he knew very well the location of the fire. What I did not love about myself, I loathed. My heart felt like a lit match near a dry grass field. I wondered if this was the way we were both built, but then I thought this must be fifteen. My mother could smell it on me: I hoped the car would be a vehicle away from myself. On more than one occasion she had said, "I don't know what you're hoping to find. It's all suburbs. People mowing lawns. Shopping, for God's sake."

"I want to try the bigger road," I replied.

"No," he said. He shook his head. "Absolutely not."

I turned left, and the wheel bounced off the curb. My father gripped the seat. "Watch the tree! Hydrant! Truck. Truck!"

I stopped. I was headed for Livernois—a double-wide, cracked road with smashed glass and wrappers at the curbline and stores like gaunt faces. It was a road where small animals were regular casualties, and if you had the nerve to open your car door into traffic, no one could be blamed for the consequences. More than one door had been stripped off its hinges. A good-sized Buick wouldn't even slow down to give it back. My father placed his palm on his forehead.

"How can I learn if I don't try?"

My father mumbled, "Grant me the serenity to accept the things I cannot change—"

"I'll take that as a yes."

My father resigned himself to his fate. He turned on the radio, found the football game, and sat back. The announcer noted the score: 27-3.

"I don't know why you listen," I said. "They always lose."

"It's not whether you win or lose…" His voice trailed off.

"Well, they don't play the game very well either, do they?" I offered. "I mean, they suck."

"Mind the road."

During a commercial, my father took out the driving test manual from the glove compartment and asked me questions. "You are at a four-way stop with another vehicle. Who goes first, you or the guy to your left?"

"I go first?" I asked.

The game came back on. The Lions recovered the fumble and were charging through the defense.

"Well?"

"Sure," he said. "Good answer."

On 8 Mile, a car cut me off, and I slammed on the brakes. The car behind me screeched. The quarterback had made it to the 20-yard line.

"Go, go!" my dad yelled. I zoomed up and changed lanes right in front of a Cadillac.

"What are you doing?"

"Touchdown!" the announcer screamed.

"You're supposed to be helping me," I yelled.

"All right, all right. It's probably the only touchdown they'll have all season. Can't I celebrate for a minute here? Can't I have a second to rejoice?"

I slammed on the brakes to a halt on a yellow. "Go right ahead."

The driver next to my father nodded knowingly. "Driver's training?"

My father nodded back.

"Stay strong," the guy said.

Dad turned back to me. "Okay, I'll give you my undivided attention. We'll try a bigger challenge—Woodward."

"No."

Woodward was a bully of a road, with ramps and eight lanes and speed limits no one followed. A friend of mine had been beaten up in the park there—by two women. They wanted her bike. A guy cut off a truck there two weeks ago. He was shot.

"Move into the right lane."

I signaled.

"You looking for pedestrians? They have the right of way, you know. See the white walking guy all lit up there?"

"Dad, I'm not a moron."

"Of course not, Mary, of course you're not a moron." He looked around anyway. "Okay, all systems go."

A squirrel ran across the street. I braked to avoid him. I glanced over at my father. He looked so tired. He would return to work the next day, and I would begin another grim week of school, where boys called out, "Hey chunky" and teachers said, "Here's the problem; you have five minutes to find the answer." My father and I had learned to view Sunday afternoons much the same, as a last gasp, a desperate and draining hope.

"Okay, here we go. Turn right."

"I don't know," I said.

"It'll be fine."

At the green light, I turned. I didn't hit the curb, and I didn't wander between the white lines. The speed sign said thirty, but cars passed us from all around.

"Stay to the right. They have to pass you."

We drove by the fairgrounds. A month ago, they packed up all the cows and pigs. The sloping barracks were left to carry the season out with tractor pulls and liquidation sales.

Cars pressed up against me, then zoomed by. Someone honked. My father yelled, "Up yours, buddy." It was more for my benefit than the driver's. My hands were sweaty on the wheel.

A car tailed me, and I barely paid attention to a group of people waiting ahead at a bus stop.

"Uh, oh," my father said.

I thought he was talking about the car behind us, so I sped up a little. I looked in the rearview mirror. His foot hit the imaginary brake. "Stop!"

I realized then that you could capture the essence of someone in a flash: the rawness, the unearthed time.

I pieced it together. A woman had waited in the throng at the bus stop, holding a plastic bag with tongue-sized flowers on the sides and the corners all chewed up. Her hair was thick and troubled, and she wore a large, blue tweed coat with buttons like woolly saucers. The life had bled out of her face. It was the emptiness of her, as though seeing a deserted street, that ate through me. She looked at me, really saw me. The others stared up the road for their bus as though they had the power to pull it toward them, as though getting home were all that mattered.

She glanced across the road. She stepped off the curb as though walking off the edge of a building, then stood right in front of our car. She looked straight at me with the burnt-out bulbs of her eyes. She wasn't afraid, and she wasn't proud. Nothing in the space of her flinched. How trapped I was, between the rushing car behind me, the people on the curb, my father, and this woman ahead. Gas stations collapsed. Parking meters froze.

What could I do? I let go of it all. My heart banged like a radiator. I heard a strange thing from deep within me, past my heart and lungs, beyond my stomach sitting like a continent deep on the sea floor. "You want to live."

Then the voice came again and again, steady and peaceful, and strangely off the mark, since it was not me that was going to die. Wasn't it her? Something in me calmed and intensified. I turned my head and swerved into the left lane. I didn't know why I even bothered to look. I would have swerved anyway. It was all I had.

I moved too fast, and my father's forehead thudded against the side window. Cars screeched behind us. The woman stood, and for a second she looked like Moses, with all the cars parting around her.

The driver behind me pulled to the side of the road. The woman walked back onto the curb. He got out and yelled at her, but when he saw her eyes, he returned to the car and slammed the door. He saw, I imagined, a woman with nothing to lose in this world. She remained, resolute, her shoulders back, her head straight. The others at the stop had already stepped away.

"Are you okay?" Dad asked.

"I didn't see her. I would have stopped. I don't know where she came from."

"No, no," he said. "She jumped into the street. I've seen it before."

"Why would she do that?"

"Crazy, or maybe it's a scam. She gets hit and then sues you." He paused. "People do desperate things. You never know why. Not for sure." He rolled down the window.

*Desperate things.* Did the woman think we had so much money? One look at our beat-up wagon could tell anyone otherwise. Would she risk losing a leg? Having her body cut open by moving steel? Or was she possessed and needed the car to frighten away the spirits?

My father sensed my thoughts. "You did the right thing."

"But what if I'd killed her?"

"You didn't."

But that was too tenuous an answer. I could have. It all seemed too risky, too possible.

"Should we help her?"

"We can call the police when we get home."

So I drove.

"Didn't she care?"

My father shrugged. "It's the chance she was willing to take."

I sped up. My father no longer yelled "Car!" or "Stop!" and he didn't scream again when the Lions caught one in the end zone.

When the Lions scored, I looked at my father. He sat with his mouth open. I wanted to ask what was wrong, but I knew better. When we drove by the apartment buildings, the gas station, and the houses with chipped paint and boarded windows, he seemed to take them personally.

When we were a few blocks from the house, he said, "Boy, Sundays just shoot by, don't they? You barely get a hooray in, and they're gone."

He would make it home for the last part of the game. He touched his forehead, where, later, a bruise would form.

"Are you okay, Dad?"

"Fine."

He switched off the radio.

"Anyway, you did really well." And after a pause, he added, "Good job."

He turned to me and smiled in that way my father does, bright and a little apologetic. And I drove. Some leaves fell into the wind. I didn't say what I felt so deeply: past my harshness, and self-doubt, I wanted to live. We didn't talk about love, since the might of our connection seemed telepathic. I even knew what he thought, but would not say—that troubles, those quiet, still times before you get up and move on, were nothing to be ashamed of. And it was out of love that I refrained from saying: don't worry. We had both learned that lesson such a long time ago.

# Scavengers

I WAS SO insanely hot I stuck to the vinyl seat. I smelled. The Dart smelled. Neal leaned over the engine, and the way he wiggled the parts, with dull misunderstanding, made me want to kill him.

It was August 1987 in Detroit, ten months after Black Monday. Martin Luther King Jr. Boulevard splayed out, a raw nerve of dry grass patches, a liquor store, and rows of one-story projects. In a cement court between the projects, a girl jumped up and down on a metal sheet wedged between a pipe and a parking block. A woman with white hair, maybe the girl's grandmother, watched from a folding chair.

Neal let the hood drop, and it slammed like a shot. He took off his wet T-shirt, wiped his face with it, and threw it into the back seat.

"I'm calm," he said. "We are all calm in this car. Anyone who isn't calm is going to have to walk."

The temperature gauge on the dash crept from H to C. Neal slumped over the steering wheel. "Thank you, Gaw-haw-hawed."

Neal threw the car into drive and looked back quickly. An Olds '98 with a bad belt whined past.

"We're not going now, right?"

"Yes," he said. "We are going, and we are *glad* we're going."

I put my hand out the window. Even the breeze burned. This weather started things: riots, family fights, mistakes. The weatherman fried an egg on a car. I couldn't believe someone actually got paid for such work.

"We shouldn't go." I put my feet on the dashboard. "Let's just get a drink."

"You're scared."

"No, I'm not."

"There's nothing to be afraid of."

"Of course not."

"Do you think anyone will even be watching, that anyone even cares?"

I thought for a moment. "No, I don't think so."

"It's not stealing," he said. "You should know that."

It wasn't stealing, Neal reasoned, because the houses died anyway. People had been leaving the city for over two decades. Some just abandoned their homes like old cars or sweaters. No one saved them. Wasn't the worst sin letting them turn to dust unnoticed? Salvage something, that's what Neal believed. Remember, it used to be a house, a home. It used to be beautiful.

Neal and I had been late to college and late to leave. We met in a painting class at Wayne State, a mile up the road. We'd registered on a whim. Meghan studied art there with a well-known painter, who approved of her thick, bold strokes and use of cadmium red. I couldn't compete. I took literature classes, and one art studio workshop, where I ripped up some pictures I'd taken and painted scenes around them.

In one piece, I used a photograph of two men carrying a bathtub out of an abandoned house. I ripped the picture in two and glued it onto the canvas. Now the men were separated, each alone carrying half a tub, as though they carried half a puzzle. I painted doors and windows and houses all around the men. "Lovely," my instructor said. "Really good."

Neal liked it, too. He had already been reclaiming tiles and wood for years, entering through windows and unlocked back doors of abandoned houses. He described creeping through dark hallways where the stillness could break you. I had taken pictures from inside cars or from the vantage of sidewalks, where a tree trunk had split and lifted the concrete.

Two weeks into the term, Neal and I started to sit together in the art studio, dabbing expensive oil paints (with their woody, pungent odors) and forgetting the time. We'd walk down the marbled steps of Old Main, dazed by the sudden night.

Neal was tall and skinny, the rock-star skinny so popular then. He'd lean forward slightly as we walked toward The Bronx for beer and popcorn. Wayne State was a commuter campus, so at night the streets opened wide with vulnerable, quivering space, where steam rose from the manholes and people walked along the edges with determined gaits. The peaceful darkness resonated with small memories, like a walk in the autumn night along the cobblestones of Canfield. There was the wonder of walking three blocks home from classes and having the rest of the night to read and watch characters pass by on the streets below. Or the time I met a guy at a party, and we kissed on the stoop of the ABC Building while someone played "No Woman No Cry" on the stereo upstairs.

There were bad times—my car break-in two months earlier. They took my books and binder full of notes just before finals week. Or the time Frank, the Vietnam vet who walked with a cane, was shot bringing flowers to his girlfriend.

The university prided itself on "nontraditional" students, which usually meant broke. Many students took their time graduating, preferring reading and intellectual discussions to the outcomes a degree offered, such as nine-to-five jobs or mortgages, which were both traps. Everyone in Detroit knew an uncle or a brother who had been laid off by a car company during record profits. In the 80s, the entire city sat at kitchen tables trying to figure out how to pay the bills. These layoffs taught the young lessons. Always have a Plan B. Don't expect a forever job.

I paid for college working two jobs. I spent seventy-eight dollars a month in rent and had three roommates. When someone robbed the apartment (with me asleep in my room), the police said, "You're lucky to be alive." It was that kind of place.

One of my favorite professors taught contemporary theory. He said "oppression" and "rebellion" a lot. One day he came in and said, "You've got to read this." He passed out a chapter from a new book called *Chaos: Making a New Science* and read a section out loud: "The first message is that there is disorder. Physicists and mathematicians want to discover regularities. People say, *What use is disorder?* But people have to know about disorder if they are going to deal with it. The auto mechanic who doesn't know about sludge in valves is not a good mechanic."

A couple of anarchists in the class hooted. One slammed her fist on the desk. "Let's dis-order America!"

A guy in the back yelled, "Know the sludge? Hell, man, we *are* the sludge."

But all of that was over now. Neal had graduated a term before me. He didn't have full-time work because there wasn't any here. He taught a few classes and did some journalism photography. I had graduated two months ago. I worked as a part-time assistant at the newspaper.

He told me the entire block would be demolished. The bridge authority had purchased the land. The renters would move someplace else, so it would all be taken, one way or another. I shouldn't feel guilt or fear.

"When we get there, you'll see," Neal said. "It's not scary."

It was all I could do not to reach over and rip his face off. What did he know about fear? Neal had never been grabbed on the street. No one ever came up to him and said, "Hey baby, want to suck my dick? You got a nice pussy there." He never knew—couldn't possibly know—that some days you were meat.

Other times, the street mocked you: candy wrappers, Big Mac styrofoam lids, bottles, the riot fencing with the padlocks. On those days you stayed inside.

"I think you need this," Neal said.

"Need what?" A woman always had more to lose. A guy could get shot. A woman, well, I'd had friends who'd lived through worse.

"Uh-oh," he said.

"What?"

"I forgot my extra bag."

Neal used the extra bag for delicate items. His apartment was a few miles away, in southwest Detroit. We found a parking space right in front. The old man who owned the building spoke only Spanish.

Usually, the man and Neal would talk. Neal would translate later. Last week, the guy asked why we weren't married. His daughter was married with kids already, and what were we up to but hanging out all night, wasting what was good and given by God.

Now, in the car I said, "Give me a kiss." Neal did. I didn't want to be kissed. I wanted to stop this trip.

"I love you, Neal," I said. "I really love you."

Neal took my hand. "Then why do you sound like you're trying to convince yourself?"

We got out of the car. We passed the petunias and the crisp lawn up the stairs and said hello to the man. When he did not lecture, I felt as though he'd given up on us. We opened the tall wooden doors and walked into the lobby with high ceilings and overpainted moldings. I imagined the many elegant people who lived here so long ago. Maybe they wore tuxedos and ball gowns. It was a huge place, grand, even with its fading. As I walked in, I didn't want a ball gown, but I wanted something, something graceful and lovely. The back of my legs stung where I had peeled them away from the Dart's vinyl seat. I'd worn shorts. That was a mistake.

Upstairs, I sat on the old rocking chair. The room felt cool. He gave me a beer.

"I'll just be a sec," he said.

I had dubbed Neal's apartment *The Land of Misfit Toys*. Things didn't fit: A faux Tiffany lamp and a Buddha with a clock in its belly, a mannequin, and a reupholstered chaise lounge. A row of velvet red seats from the closed Palms Theatre. A Miles Davis picture next to a poster of Archie Bunker with "I like Nixon" printed on the bottom. Saved, every one of them, from homes, alleys, and garage sales.

We had talked of leaving—moving out to the suburbs. But the dullness there, the facelifts, the big cars, the neighborhoods without sidewalks, was a threat to sanity, to art. I'd applied for a grant-writing job in the suburb of Birmingham.

"You might as well apply someplace in North Carolina," Neal said. "People are that different. They walk around with rods up their asses and talk about their investments."

When I put my hand out the window, my fingers rippled. "Sounds painful."

"You have no idea."

Seeing Neal's fervor that day made me understand. Neal would never leave. He saw himself as an amateur archaeologist. He liked living this way. The list-makers, as he called them, the capitalists, frightened Neal at first, and then only reminded him of a life avoided, numbed by products. I knew, too, that such a world collected piece by piece—the new car, a house, with a lawn to mow—would kill the best part of him. Often, living here meant humor and oddity, a real experience. But how to get through the bad days, the heat and the dirt, how to get through those times that threatened to swallow you, proved impossible. On those days (days like this one), a broken-down car or one wrong move could lead to an avalanche of consequences. They were everywhere. The drugs. Jesus, the vials and the bullet casings and the shots in the night. Anyone could slide. Anyone.

But opportunities could arise. My boss said a full-time assistant job had opened in another department. He would put in a good word for me. I wanted the security, but not the monotony, not the nine-to-five everyday forever. A reporter would be something, but the two newspapers hired Ivy League graduates, people from other places who would go on to other places. Who was I to refuse a job as assistant? No, I would take it, because I didn't want to choose anymore between gasoline and groceries, between money for rent and money for clothes. Because people in this city were starving. It could happen to me. I wasn't arrogant enough to think otherwise.

I studied some smaller pictures Neal had framed. "Margaret Thatcher is too much," I said. "Take her down."

"Really? I thought it added a little femininity."

I studied Thatcher's face. "Nixon is more feminine."

"Huh." Neal paused to observe the piece.

"It's too late now," I said. "Let's go tomorrow."

"We can make it." Neal grabbed the extra bag and his keys. He kissed my neck. "Well, *I* love *you*."

He locked the door, and we walked downstairs and out onto West Grand Boulevard. The church bells rang eight times, and the air still languished in gasoline exhaust and sweat. We slipped into the car, and I put my feet on the dash, so my legs wouldn't stick. I hadn't brought mace, which seemed useless anyway. In the time it took to turn the safety latch, a robbery would be over. Once I'd accidentally left the latch open and maced myself trying to unlock my apartment door. Meghan thought that was hilarious. She added, "I wouldn't need mace. I could kill a guy with my bare hands."

When I told that to Neal, he shook his head and tried not to laugh. "Weaponry is not your specialty."

Neal, Meghan, and I were born here, and, like most people here, we'd all been robbed several times. I knew that when you were in that moment, you didn't know what you would do. Your mind took over. You had to be ready.

Now I had keys, and they could gouge an eye out. I made a fist, the keys popping out between my fingers. My firm grip kept the keys from slipping.

We turned left on the street just before the Ambassador Bridge to Canada, where cars and trucks idled in long lines. Pollution from gasoline exhaust and Rouge River refineries hung over the bridge in a haze. We drove two blocks farther into a neighborhood. Kids played in the yard of the first corner house. Grass and weeds grew on empty lots there, and between those lots were two-story brick houses. No matter how bad the decay, we always noticed that one house on every block looked pristine, with fresh paint and flowers. As we drove by two such houses in a row, we wanted to knock on their doors and ask the owners how they maintained such grace and dignity. The remaining brick and wood houses had the telltale signs of abandonment: dark rooms, windows without curtains, without glass.

Neal turned right. I thought I saw the house. Plywood covered the windows and door. It was followed by an empty lot.

"We'll never get in," I said.

"That's not it." Neal passed the third house, then the fourth, and parked just before the fifth house.

I looked back. This couldn't be right. Someone had cut that lawn, maybe even that day. The windows were big, and unbroken. Flowers grew in the yard.

"Someone lives here."

"The neighbors do it," he said. "To throw people off."

We put on black baseball caps and jackets with hoods. I'd forgotten my black pants at home. I had to risk the nails and splinters. We walked to the corner then through the alley.

Police prioritized murders, robberies, and domestic incidents. Neighbors watched, so you had to slip in. I'd heard of one angry neighbor who lived near an abandoned house where squatters sold drugs. The man lit a match, threw it inside a broken window, and watched the people scatter. Half an hour later, the house engulfed, the fire department came.

"Hurry," I said. I felt thirsty.

No one was standing in the alley, and no one jumped out unexpectedly. We walked by the garage and through the yard. The color of the leaves had already dulled.

Neal walked up to the side of the house and lifted a window open as far as he could. The window was five feet above ground. Neal threaded his fingers together and motioned for me to put my foot there. "You first."

I thought once more of calling it off, but we had come this far. I put my right foot in first, wavered, and fell back on my other foot. The second time I grabbed hold of the window right away and up I went, hip on the sill, turning carefully to avoid the nails. I jumped in and took Neal's bag. He braced his arms on the sides of the window and climbed up and in. I smelled fall in the leaves. The house was cooled by the shade-giving trees. The bright greens there had begun to soften a bit, as they did in the boiling August days here. It wouldn't be long.

We turned around and surveyed the dining room, with wooden floors and pink walls. White curtains hung in the windows. Neal hit the light switch. "See? Power's off."

Wood covered the doors, the arches, and the floor. A dewdrop glass fixture hung from a sconce on the wall. Stairs leading to the second floor were detailed with honey-colored wood banisters engraved with flowers. This place was a home, I thought. Someone should save this, not the parts but the entirety.

"Somebody's already started," Neal said. "They already took the French doors."

He stared at the hinges in disappointment. We looked around. The sink in the bathroom had also been ripped out. "Let's hurry."

There was so much more to take, so many reasons for people to come back.

Neal wanted the tiles above the fireplace. He told me to get the fixtures—the small antique ones brought in the real money. He showed me how to take the one in the hall first. He pressed a screwdriver into the wall and twisted. Then he pulled out the sconce and cut the thick wires. Neal took the bubble wrap from his extra bag, wrapped the fixture, and then tucked it into the bag.

I grabbed the screwdriver and the shears and walked upstairs. From the hall, I saw three bedrooms and a bathroom. But I turned around to look again at a beautiful crystal light piece hanging on the wall at the top of the stairs. It had silver arms that rolled down into a half-circle of three candles with wire-wick bulbs. Crystal dewdrop facets hung under the candles, and the entire piece was laced with crystal beads. It was a stunning design, something that cried out to be saved. The screws turned easily, and I pulled the fixture out. The wires were thick and hard to cut. I had forgotten Neal's bag downstairs, so I carried it into the nearby bedroom. The morning-yellow wallpaper with little purple violets looked new. A stuffed dolphin lay abandoned in the corner. I wondered if I would ever own a home, if I would ever be like the family who once lived here. Surely, they had been a family. This place resonated with hopes and childhood. But something had gone terribly wrong, someone laid off, or an illness discovered. And then they were cast out into the street like so many here. How cruel it all was. How unforgiving.

Since I didn't see any light fixtures in the other rooms, I walked into the largest bedroom and looked up. I saw an oval ceiling light, as big as a platter, with lines and small droplets of crystal around the bulbs. I glanced out the window. The sunset reflected on the houses across the street. I saw the Ambassador Bridge, and the pale moon in a blue sky. I smelled liquor.

Maybe I could afford a house in Neal's neighborhood, and maybe I could fix it up. Maybe this fixture could go in my new house. I wanted it then—the fixture and that life. I wanted it with a yearning so fresh and raw, it hurt.

Then I saw him. At first I thought he might be a ghost or a projection of my fears. He was crouched in the closet, looking at me. He had a beard, and his eyes were wild. Starving. A few plastic grocery bags lay scattered around him. A blanket was spread out. He held a Wild Irish Rose bottle. He had been, I knew then, keeping quiet, hoping not to be seen, or deciding what to do. I put my hand in my pocket and grabbed the keys, clenching them in my fist. I felt life rushing through me.

I sussed him out. Could I take him? Did I need to? His eyes opened wide. It could be harmless. But the people we knew had told cautionary tales, tales of being too nice, of waiting too long, of responding to help, just before they were attacked. They told us this, risking shame, to warn us.

Women I knew sat at bars or in dark rooms or at coffee shops and poured their lives out, in relief, in warning. Don't go down that road at night. Don't date a guy who puts you on a pedestal. It is a long way down and it ends in a crash. I listened as they said, "Offend someone if you must, but get away." As I thought this, it was already too late.

He stood up. "I was just sleeping here." He sounded like a parent comforting a troubled child. He walked toward me. "I was just sleeping."

I did not step back. This man wanted a home, too, I reasoned. He just wanted to be left alone. That's what the man was trying to convey.

But why was he moving toward me? Everyone who was robbed or attacked had a piece of advice: don't be a girl.

I yelled down the warning phrase we'd practiced: "Neal, get the gun! Get the gun!"

I heard a loud boom, which was also part of the plan. It jarred the man. We were trapped. We didn't know, either of us, what the other would do. Maybe we were both peaceful, maybe it would be all right. I still wanted to believe he was kind and lost.

"I've got the gun!" Neal screamed. He kept on screaming, in a voice deep and guttural, up the stairs.

The man moved back into the corner. "I'm just sleeping I'm just sleeping!"

Neal charged up the stairs, a wrench in one hand and a hammer in the other. He pulled me out of the doorway. He ran into the room.

The man sat in the corner. He smelled like earth, sweat, and fear. He had a few layers of clothes on, and I imagined they were all the clothes he owned. He must be so hot, I thought. He yelled, and ran past Neal, past me, out the door, down the stairs, and he was gone. Neal and I went to the window, but we couldn't see him. We ran to the window in the main bedroom and saw the man walking quickly, trying not to attract attention.

"Let's go, let's go," I said. I gripped the sconce. How could I have held it the entire time? Now I held the piece to my chest, as though the fixture was my life, and ran down the stairs. Neal followed.

In the kitchen, I heard Neal say, "He's gone. Hold up. He's gone."

But I kept going. I would run all the way home. He didn't understand. It wasn't just a man. It wasn't just a house. It was all wrong: our theft, his squatting, the government, the corporations. Whatever made this situation was wrong.

The man could have just wanted to sleep there. He could have been a nice guy. Or he could have gone to get his friends. I took off, down the back stairs, through the yard, through the alley, and to the car. I ran so fast I had to wait by the car for Neal to catch up. Down the street I saw cars parked and abandoned and a factory smokestack beyond some trees. A man with a child watched from their stoop. This was wrong, feeding off the carcass of the remains. What did we show that kid? That his neighborhood was only worth the pieces that were hauled away?

We got in the car. When I set the fixture down at my feet, the crystals tinged together. Neal drove two blocks then pulled over on a dead corner.

"Are you okay?"

I nodded, but I couldn't feel anything outside my body. My heart raced. My legs tingled. I was alive. But I couldn't feel anything past that—not the heat and not the day. I pulled my legs up to my chest and held them there. I bit my knee.

Neal drove another block. It was abandoned except for one house. On the next block, house lights beamed. We passed the bridge with the long lines of trucks and cars trying to get into Canada. Then we drove toward Neal's apartment.

Past Bagley, someone flew by on his bike. Neal swerved in time. It was a kid. He didn't look back. I wondered who might be in the houses and apartments we passed. What might be happening? Was it true that a gesture in a second changed everything? Was this Chaos Theory, happening now?

The lights, so many lives, came and went in flashes, but I couldn't look, so I turned to Neal and saw the streetlights reflect off him. How golden he looked, how the breeze hit his hair. I put my palm on his arm.

"I love you," I said. A dark patch came and then lights. I felt a sharp pain, like something had been plucked. I placed my palm to my stomach, but when I pressed my fingers there, I couldn't name the feeling that had been taken, like a dream or a wish; something that, once you named it, was already gone.

# The Leisure Class

ERIN WAS MY best friend in the world. The only one I could trust. So when she called to say, "I'm having a party," I responded, "Don't do it."

We were wild things then, Erin especially, with her basketball height and lean body galloping over the buckling, cracked streets of southwest Detroit. Erin feared nothing, because she came from the rebel clan—a black father, a white mother, a rich family, a poor family—a mix so potent strangers couldn't figure her out. I was terribly proud to walk with her, to watch people gawk as if she were a famous person they couldn't quite place. Erin's neighbors, who rented floors in duplexes, or occupied abandoned mansions and painted walk-ups, looked out for Erin because she had no man and no kids, a grievous situation for which they would light Our Lady of Guadalupe candles and leave tamales and loaves of warm bread on her stoop.

Erin said "Much obliged," but told me later she didn't need looking after or prayers because she was 6'5" and no one dared to fuck with a woman of such height. Surely the neighbors saw how Erin treated herself—cigarettes for breakfast and coney dogs for lunch, when she could scrape up the cash from what wasn't handed out to people she loved.

Her parties always ended up with drunken brawls, with cops coming, or with someone nearly OD'ing and then crashing at her place for a month. I refused to go last time, but my one-woman protest was useless. Out of guilt, I showed up the next morning to help clean.

When I called to talk her out of the party, Erin responded in the tone of a dare. "Like you'll come anyway."

She exhaled her cigarette smoke and awaited my rebuttal.

I had none. I had to go to the party to protect her from her own family and bad friends like Lottie. Plus, I had to talk to Erin about my plan.

We met in an art class at the city college. After we graduated, Erin still painted five nights a week. I was in month six of a break from painting. I blamed the job.

"I'll be there. I need to talk to you."

"Yeah?" She exhaled her cigarette. "About what?"

"It's complicated."

"You? Complicated? Wow. What a shock."

"I'm showing up. And I'm bringing my knife to fight off the criminal element."

"Good, you'll need it." She hung up.

It was just a dumb trip to England. I was going with an old friend. We'd been to Ireland two years before. We went on the cheap—youth hostels and cold rain; hiking and Guinness. So we planned a trip to England. But after a month of researching routes and plane tickets, she stopped cold at youth hostels. She wanted hotels. Friends joined in.

"We're graduated now," she said. "We can afford it."

They could afford it. They planned shopping destinations. They invited me to a party. They drank champagne from glasses with long stems. They said, "That's cute." Over and over, they said this.

At the party, I looked to my wine glass and caught sight of my Salvation Army skirt. I saw my worn boots and noticed, for the first time, their new clothes: bright prints, scarves in their hair; some with gold bracelets.

I should have known. Even in college, when my roommates and I stole toilet paper from Old Main and lived on noodles. The England-bound crew wore jeans ripped by designers and worked in family businesses.

The sparkling wine went down easily. I had to think fast to save myself. No matter how I planned and saved, this "trip of a lifetime" would tip me into poverty and debt. Erin would know how to fix it. Erin would tell me how to get out of it without shame. "Fuck 'em," I could hear her say. So what if I told a little lie with Erin in the middle? She didn't like these people.

On the night of Erin's party, I booked it over to Walnut Lane and found a spot down the road, between a Fairmont and a Dart. Cups and a couple of whiskey bottles were already tossed under Erin's massive oak tree. Its thick roots lifted the sidewalk. The overgrown limbs lazed on her roof.

In the basement I tried to mingle with her bow-legged and rakish aunties, who teetered along the cement floor toward me, their gray hair hanging like shorn curtains. Only the poor rellies showed up at Erin's parties. Erin said her dad's clan was too stuck up, but I sensed her uncle's job as a state representative kept them away. The man couldn't be caught in pictures with felons.

"So how do you know our Erin?" one woman asked me, as she leaned against the other.

"College," I said. "She's a great painter."

"Damn straight," said Uncle Shane. He wore his Vietnam vet shirt with the saying "Brotherhood Can't be Bought Must be Earned." He gripped a support pole, his leather jacket squeaking with every inhale of his Pall Mall. He took a fifth of Jack Daniel's from his inside coat pocket and gave it to the other auntie, who said, "Thank you kindly, sir," and took a swig.

To look at them would make anyone nervous about Erin's biracial identity. But the last time a guy asked Erin "what the hell" she was, Uncle Shane beat the crap out of him. The guy lost two teeth.

"She's our godsen'," the other auntie said. I wanted to say, "You mean Godsend." But I held my tongue.

"She's helped you a lot," I said. "I know."

They all nodded. Uncle Shane hacked and lit another Pall Mall.

Erin's high school friends started trickling in. Her painter friends wouldn't make it until after the Michigan Gallery closed, or Angry Red Planet finished their set at Alvin's.

We called them tribes. I had my pack with Erin and a couple of artists yet to arrive. Lottie's band, the Three Thieves, strolled in first. I gave them the title after a house-stripping incident. They liked the insult so much they named their band after it. Shit. Those phonies even stole insults.

The Three Thieves included Lottie, a drummer, and her boyfriend, who blathered on about how their music was "avant-garde, really before its time." They used their unsung hero status as an excuse to drink so much of the house beer their guts swelled, and their legs became rubbery and unfaithful. They kept one hand on the wooden ceiling beams above them.

Lottie wore a faded flower print dress with Doc Martens and one white sock lifted higher than the other, like she was that kid holding a grenade in the Diane Arbus picture. She wore the outfit to look innocent, a naïve girl amidst the wreckage of our town and her boyfriend, who couldn't stop flirting with women and men, a mannequin, a support beam—it didn't matter. Lottie played the fiddle. Her boyfriend, Donny, was the band percussionist, which meant he tinged a triangle, or tapped a cowbell while nodding with his eyes half-closed, like he might pass out from his own brilliance. Donny smiled as their drummer, Cocho, followed a married woman up the basement stairs and into trouble.

Thirty minutes in and I'd had it. I wasn't the only one with friend problems. I found a spot on the gnawed plaid couch between a mannequin and Erin's dog, Ralphie, who proceeded to lap beer from my red plastic cup. The only view I had of the party was an ass and a gut that hung down over Donny's half-open zipper. Those fuckers knew how to obstruct a view.

Erin had put the keg downstairs; that was the problem. The more people drank, the more they believed they'd always belonged in this basement with its earthy smell and darkness of a collective grave.

Erin, tall and reed-thin, no hips whatsoever, still worked her way through the crowd. She'd shaved the side of her head. Erin's sleek agility amidst the others made her look like a gazelle in a psych ward. I tilted over and lifted my arm to get Erin's attention. Erin put her index finger up, the universal sign for wait a minute.

"Ralphie," she yelled. Ralphie sprang from the couch, leaving a free spot. Down plopped Donny, sinking so hard into the rusty coils that I tilted straight toward him until we pressed shoulder to shoulder.

I lifted myself closer to the mannequin, whose bony elbow ate into my back. Donny started mouth breathing, then finally thought of something to say. "Hey, sorry about that. I just need a sit, if you know what I mean."

I kept pushing myself back up against the mannequin's elbow. "How's the band, Donny?"

"We're opening for the Leisure Class at Paycheck's on Friday. You should come. I'll get you on the list."

"How'd you score that?"

"The bar manager and I both love that band."

"Isn't that funny? You know, on stage you move a lot like the percussion guy from the Leisure Class, with your tambourine solo and all."

Damn it if Donny hadn't stolen the persona outright.

Donny smiled like he'd been waiting months for someone to notice the connection. "It was a triangle solo. I do believe it was the first triangle solo ever attempted in North America. Besides, imitation's the best form of flattery."

I looked around at people pushing and shoving each other playfully. The room resembled an ER unit, with skinny-legged cirrhosis patients hacking like asthmatics, their fingers jabbing the air to make critical points. How many people in this room were wanted by police? Donny, for example, had already been arrested once for stealing a car, which he blamed on prescription meds, thereby obstructing the view of the true facts.

This basement wasn't my life, but neither were English hotels and "cute" things. I wanted the world of urban thrift, of going to shows at happy hour, long before the cover charge, of finding deals that screwed the system, of the tribes living off the greed grid. I studied the floor, the room.

Lottie walked by and said, "You painting, Mary?"

It felt like a jab in the gut. "Not really."

I thought about youth hostels and backpacks. In Ireland people lived in a collective poverty, walking on cobblestones and wrapping their heads in shawls. I counted every penny there, ate bread with slabs of butter for lunch, and loved the hard, wet wind against my face as we walked the dirt road to the Giant's Causeway.

Erin was my excuse for not going to England. At the wine party, I tried honesty. "I can't afford an expensive trip." But they wouldn't listen.

One woman said, "Go into debt. Buy beautiful, rare things, and meet men at cafés."

Another woman said, "Oh, come on. Go with us. Money isn't everything."

I froze. I'd paid for college myself, bought used clothes, and kept within a budget. I'd lived on boxed macaroni and cheese to keep debts down. So now, after all my creative and gritty resourcefulness, I'm supposed to argue with people who'd never worried about money in their lives? No. I couldn't expose myself that way. I moved on to Plan B.

"I'm too busy with the band," I said.

"What band?" she asked.

"The band with Erin," I said. "We've got a few shows coming up, so we really have to practice."

"Huh. Well I want to see this band. Let me know the dates. We'd all love to see you play."

*Shit.*

Now, Erin sauntered over. "Incoming," she said and sat on me and Donny. We both shoved over to make room. "Well," Erin said. "This is cozy."

"I've got to talk to you," I said. "It's urgent."

"Okay. Beat it, Donny."

"Don't mind if I do," he said, with a disgusting smile on his face.

She flipped him off. "Gross."

He heaved himself up, leaning so far over that his butt cracked open like a corpse flower.

"Jesus," Erin said. "Thanks for the show."

Erin put her arm around me. "What's so wrong?"

"You and me, we're forming a band, okay?"

Erin narrowed her eyes and hit on her cigarette. "Yeah? What do I play?"

"You look like a singer to me."

"What do you play?"

"Guitar. Sort of."

"Okay let me ask you something." Erin turned her head to the room and yelled, "Hey, Jason, can you let Ralphie in?"

I didn't know Jason. But he looked like all the other guys, with his thin frame and glassy eyes.

"He's mine," Erin said, as she watched Jason walk upstairs. "So, where've you been?"

"What'd you mean?"

"I mean, I haven't seen you in months and now you show up and you want us to be in a band."

I blinked. "I've been hanging out with the wrong crowd."

"Who?"

"You know. Turns out I'm not going to England. They're going to shop."

Erin rolled her eyes. "The nose jobbers." One of them had had a nose job. Another lived in a house rumored to have a stream running through it. Her family made their money from selling overpriced iceberg lettuce in their urban stores.

The soft couch made my skirt ride up, so I lifted my butt and pulled down the hem. "You were right. I was wrong."

One of Erin's aunts came up, and said, "Hey, girl, I've got to go." Erin's aunt gave her this great smile, sincere and big, and it wasn't marred that much by the missing teeth. She bent down, and Erin kissed her. Her aunt stumbled.

"You want some coffee?" Erin asked.

Her aunt got a serious look to her face and swatted the air. "You know me. I drive better when I'm drunk."

"Right on," Erin said.

I nudged her. "See? You hang with the wrong people, too."

"No, I don't."

"Anyway, we're a band. We rehearse on Thursdays."

"I can't make Thursdays."

"Why not?"

"I go to Lottie's on Thursdays. We knit."

"Fuck knitting."

Erin's eyes narrowed, which was a spectacular thing to witness. That look had wilderness in it: carcasses and long, brutal winters.

"Okay, what about Tuesday?" I had to work the other nights, and Erin worked days.

Erin studied me. "You're strange, man."

"Why?"

I straightened my hem again. People near me drank tequila. Uncle Shane fell on the floor and a guy helped him up.

"Uncle Shane, are you okay?" Erin said.

"I'm good," Uncle Shane said. He'd fallen near a steel pole. He had to hold the thing to get up, and kept hanging on, even as he stood, as if the whole world tipped around him, and only he knew.

Erin said, "Tell you what, if you really want to form a band, and you're serious about it, and you'll stick with it, then call me tomorrow and we'll talk."

Erin got up. Her aunt gave her a bottle of Jack. Erin took a gulp and walked into the crowd.

What the hell was that supposed to mean? What kind of friendship was this? Did I seem like a woman who made up and dumped ideas? Did I seem like a ne'er-do-well?

Uncle Shane leaned on Donny.

"Whoa, buddy. Hang in there now."

"You're all right," Uncle Shane said, slapping Donny's back. "You're one of the good guys."

Donny plopped down next to me again. It wasn't just Donny. I was irritated by the knitting, and Uncle Shane, and Aunt Drunk Driver. Soon, one of these people would do Erin damage.

Jason came back downstairs. Erin smoked a cigarette and slapped Jason's arm. He was too short for her, and the way she leaned over him, like a Great Dane sniffs a beagle, should clue anyone into the madness. Not Erin, though. She downed a shot someone gave her, and they walked up the stairs. I planned to split then, but Lottie came stomping up in her thick shoes and a look of fury on her face. She charged up on Donny and said, "Donny, fuck you and fuck all of your other girls."

I turned to find Donny, his zipper all the way open now, and his dick hard, pressing on his grundies. Who was he hard on? He could have been looking at someone else, but Donny was sitting next to me. I jumped up from the couch.

"Jesus," I yelled. "Donny, you are one gross motherfucker."

Donny shrugged and raised his palms to the sky. "I'm in good spirits."

He got up to talk to Lottie, but as soon as he hoisted himself out of the seat, Lottie hit him.

Watching someone get hit wasn't like in the movies. As Lottie pulled her fist back, the movements slowed. My shock muffled out the other noise. When her fist hit his face, I cringed at the sound of flesh hitting bone. It was an awful thud, a dead noise, like two carcasses knocking together in a meat plant. The impact sent Donny back on the couch. He grabbed his jaw, and my stomach clenched.

Lottie cried. Donny said over and over again, "I was just happy." And then he passed out.

People gasped. Someone yelled, "Get water."

"Call an ambulance."

"Don't call an ambulance, we'll all be arrested."

"Get water."

Erin must have heard the commotion. She came running down the stairs with water, and someone took it and threw it on Donny. He woke up, made the sign of the cross, and said, "In nomine Patris, et Filii, et Spiritus Sancti."

"Amen, Father Donny," Erin said.

Half the room bowed their heads and two guys spit on the ground. Erin said, "I can't leave for one minute."

She turned and walked toward the keg.

Lottie helped Donny up, and they stood together like lovebirds. I sat down briefly thinking to myself, *I've got to get the hell out of here before someone gets killed.*

I heard Uncle Shane yell, "Watch it." I looked up, but couldn't see the view for Lottie and Donny.

I heard a pop like a rogue firework and then thought, *Did it get darker in here?* A group of people gathered around Erin and she said, "Look, I'm fine."

"Holy crap, did you see that?" Donny asked.

"Calm down. I'm good," Erin said.

People were stunned for about thirty seconds. Someone lit a cigarette, another went for a beer. The party chatter resumed.

Erin went upstairs and snapped back, "I don't need your help."

Good for Erin, I thought. They were meddlesome, and needy, and she probably wanted some space. If Erin said leave her alone, she meant leave her alone.

Lottie propped Donny against the wall and ran upstairs.

I felt something wet. From that couch the water roused an aroma of parties and dark, terrible days. I got up.

It seemed to me that Erin belonged to a ravenous people, and if we didn't stay together, we'd be used up, or killed for our meat. If you wanted to survive in this world, you had to keep a little feral. You had to keep moving.

With Erin gone, I didn't know anyone besides Donny, whose head was veering from side to side, making a sing-song point to himself. I didn't have anyone to say goodbye to. It was weird, all through college I had plenty of friends, but graduation was like cops showing up at the party. Everyone scattered.

I walked out with a lonely feeling, and said, "No, no I'll start the band, and we'll meet people, because we'll be on stage. It'll be good." I slipped past Ralphie, who waited at the front door, and looked at me as if to say, "It's okay, they let me outside all of the time." I missed the other artists, but by then, it didn't matter.

Cocho, the drummer, walked back in with the married woman who had snuck away from her husband. I slipped out as the biggest fight of the night would soon begin.

When I got home, my England-bound friend left a message on my phone. "It's not too late to come with us. Call me."

The next morning, I woke up thinking about England. I thought I should get out of town for a while. Clear my head. I counted all the money I had, which was only a few hundred dollars. Everyone was going into debt. Why did I think my case was so special?

But I thought of what Erin might say: "You'll go to another country and be rejected by the same people who dismissed you here." Or, "You're going to the place that created punk with the most unpunk people you know."

All this made me think not of England, but of Erin. I had a bad feeling.

I waited until noon, then called her place.

A woman answered.

"Erin?"

"No, this is Lottie. Who's this?" Lottie sounded like a sailor, with her raspy smoker's voice.

"It's Mary. Is Erin all right?"

"She's fine. Look, I don't need you messing with Donny. All right?"

Donny had hit on *me*, but I didn't want to remind her.

"You can have him, Lottie. He's not my type." I hoped for sincerity.

Lottie shot back, "Oh, so now you're too good for him."

I wanted Lottie out of the tribe. She couldn't be in the band or near the band. This would be a new clan of people. No crazies, even if she played a mean fiddle.

"Can I talk to Erin?"

"She can't talk."

I stopped breathing for a second. "She asleep?"

"After she sheered that light bulb she went upstairs and passed out on the bed."

85

"What light bulb?"

I couldn't hear. I saw the lamp, a Tiffany rip-off I'd gotten for twenty dollars at a garage sale. I saw my cat asleep on the couch. The neighbor was cooking with onions next door.

"Duh. She walked right into the light bulb. You were there. You left right after."

Lottie said the bulb shattered, and light sprayed all over the ceiling.

"Oh no."

"I pulled the pieces out of her head last night."

"Holy shit."

"She can't talk now, is the thing. Call her later, if you want."

"Okay."

I hung up.

How had I missed it? I sat with my hand on the phone for some time, trying to make sense of the details. The light went dim. Erin told people to leave her alone. I wanted out. I remembered that.

Later, Erin said that she heard a crash and the tinkle of effervescent glass hitting the concrete flooring that tipped, from every end, toward the drain. I heard only people talking over one another.

The guilt sickened me. Another friend, Lottie, stayed with Erin until the morning. Another friend waited until the sad, strong sun heaved itself over the creaking houses with the tree limbs sagging outside her window. I imagined the wind swirling the leaves along the streets until they caught under bald tires of parallel-parked junkers. Another friend made Erin sit on a chair, her head tipped like Ralphie, eyes closed, mouth hanging open, as she pulled out, piece after piece, shards of glass so small they looked like spears held in the haunches of ants.

I put my coat on and then grabbed two apples. I got in the car. The gas gauge hovered above E, but I could make it.

I drove down to Michigan Ave., made a right and took that into Erin's neighborhood. I had to circle twice but found a parking space two blocks over. I put a credit card through the lock, and the door sprang open.

As I walked upstairs, the screen door banged, so I knew Lottie was out back smoking.

"Erin, it's Mary, I'm coming in."

"Leave me alone."

I knew Erin didn't want to be seen this way, hungover and unkempt. Maybe it was a mistake to come. But I knocked, opened the door, and walked into her bedroom anyway, because there were worse mistakes.

Ralphie ran in and sprang up on the bed.

"Piss off, Mary," Erin said, like she meant it.

I stayed calm and walked toward Erin like nothing was out of the ordinary. "Okay. I'll piss off."

Erin couldn't see it. Blood had dribbled down and encrusted her forehead, her shoulders, and her neck.

Of course Lottie hadn't gotten it all. Of course she didn't clean Erin off. They had both been drunk.

Lottie came upstairs and said, "I heard voices."

I grabbed Lottie by the arm and whispered, "Get a dark towel with warm water."

Lottie stared at Erin like she might throw up. "Lottie, come on." I put on my calm face.

"Does it look bad?" Erin asked.

The pillow, the sheets, and her hair were speckled with blood. It seemed to have rained from the ceiling.

"No, not bad. We just have to get a few pieces out that they didn't see in the night. Lottie and I are doing this together. She's coming with a cloth."

"Here I am." Lottie came in, upbeat, and sat by Erin while I pulled out piece one, piece two, piece three. When I pulled out the pieces, only a little fresh blood came up, one blob and then another, and then Lottie could wipe away what had crusted over.

We searched and plucked shards of glass for some time, an hour maybe, because we had to check the scalp and get everything clean, otherwise she could get an infection. Ralphie licked Erin's hand as a comfort.

I gave Erin one of the two apples. I took a bite of the second, just to break the skin, and gave the second apple to Ralphie, because he liked to chew on the meaty insides. Erin had a thing for them, and Ralphie liked everything Erin liked, including beer, apples, and running down alleys.

"Ralphie, you are my little wonder dog," Erin said.

We all said, "Ralphie," repeatedly, in high and low voices, until he wagged his tail and jumped for joy.

"Is it okay? Tell me the truth."

"Your forehead was a cactus," Lottie said.

"Actually," I said, studying it. "You were pretty lucky Lottie got the bigger pieces out right away."

Erin's forehead had four small gashes. After that, there were little pricks where shards had imbedded. It made me think about the way life heals—the way it looks so bad, and then it isn't.

Erin had been studying me. "Go to England," she said. It came out of nowhere, a command more than a plea.

"You're hungover."

"You belong with them," Erin said.

"That's mean," I said.

Erin started to cry. "Shit."

How could Erin miss it? I felt my hands getting clammy. A shiver passed through me. How long had I hung around that England-bound crew and felt the same? How could we not see the best of what we were?

I looked around the room. Her paintings, big and bold, hung everywhere. "Hey, at least you're painting. That's better than me."

"You're not painting?"

Other than Lottie at the party, no one had asked me that in a long time. "No. We're starting a band today," I said. "You and me, we're the founding members."

"Can I be in it?" Lottie asked.

I looked at Erin.

"No Donny," Erin said, wiping her eyes. She pointed at me. "And you have to start fucking painting again—today. No excuses."

I nodded. It was weird. An electrical current coursed through me. My sister Meghan was the real artist. I was just dabbling. But Erin's demand changed that. I felt anointed; blessed by Erin, the Madonna of the Holy Sheering. I was an artist again. My shoulders relaxed. My eyes watered. I didn't know why exactly. I didn't care. The sun cast shadows off the tree limbs and across the room. It was as though I were in the basement of the house, a little under the ground, smelling the earth. I didn't want to go to England. I wanted a Europe of the mind. Every day, no matter what, I would go there. They could take jobs, trips, and money, but they couldn't get this. What I created was mine to cherish and nurture, every day, for the rest of my life.

I told Erin to stand up for a second, and just in time, before she could ask why, I pulled off the blood-stained sheets, so Erin couldn't see it and go all Three Mile Island.

I walked downstairs with the linens in a bundle. The blood would never come out. I passed the booze bottles and red cups on the kitchen counters. I opened the back door and let Ralphie fly past me, prancing and sniffing with glee. He peed on the fence and kicked his hind feet against the grass. I opened the sheets on the ground and folded the bloody parts in first, so Erin couldn't walk out to the trash and see the part of herself that got away.

Ralphie followed me to the trash. I lifted the lid and pressed the sheets into the full bin. I saw the alley with the red bricks sinking and dipping where the weight of cars carved ruts. On the alley's edges, bushes grew here and there, untrimmed and funny. Someone drove through in a red Buick with a rusty fender. I didn't know the guy, but as he put his right palm up without an actual wave, I smiled at the signature of everything in this town, like all the mayhem and the crazies required you to be more of yourself, to sink your roots deep into the earth until you became trees, uplifting parts of sidewalks with robust fortitude. I felt a bursting warmth. The alley looked like a painting. I raised my palm, kept my wrist stiff and moved my hand back and forth slowly, like I was a queen in a procession. With that final gesture, I said hello to the stranger, to this alley, to this life, and goodbye to the people of England.

# The Gods of Jackson

THAT SUMMER, WHEN the lawns burst into flames, I packed some clothes and my Irish mythology books and rented a room from a farmer's daughter named Eunice in Jackson, Michigan. I had been hired as an intern at a newspaper, where I wrote stories about a drought that scalded crops and ravaged family farms.

A week after I moved in, Eunice and I ate dessert in front of the picture window, and Eunice told me how she had left her husband.

"He beat me," she said. Eunice wore whipped hair, gray and high, styled once a week. She sewed all of her own A-line dresses. "So I squirreled away a dollar here, a dollar there."

As the night came on, a ball of fire ignited in front of the corner house and then smoldered dead.

"Didn't it take forever?" I asked.

"Seven years." Eunice scooped up the rest of her cobbler, licked her spoon, and smiled, comforted by the sweetness. Two maples shaded the front of the house. In the day's broiling heat, she'd keep the windows closed and curtains drawn to hold in the cool air.

The drought forced a water shortage. The government banned lawn watering, so residents in town abandoned their yards, and the blades turned tan as wheat. Three days earlier, a man had walked by, flicked a cigarette butt, and *whoosh*, the lawn next door rolled away in a wave of flames.

At night, Eunice opened the shades and windows. It was too dark to see people, but when we heard a snap, then a burst, we looked out to a quick ball of fire that seemed to come from the blades themselves, as if they were monks protesting the war.

"Kids," Eunice said. "It's a game now. They're sneaking out into the night with matches."

I didn't tell Eunice my own story. I was ashamed of it. Before I left Detroit, I'd gotten back together with Paul. He lived illegally in his art studio downtown. We saw local bands, stayed up all night talking, and split falafel plates at a diner on Warren.

Then he showed up drooling, and his words came out in slow motion.

"What's wrong?" I asked then.

"Nothing," he said, with the front part of the word lasting forever.

Soon after that, he collapsed outside his studio, and I got a call from the hospital. He was headed straight to rehab for heroin. How did I miss it? How could I not see? How could I trust anything?

We had been back together for six months. When I visited him in rehab, he told me, with his head bowed, that this was his second rehab. The first one didn't take. But he was better now. Couldn't I see he was better?

I didn't want Eunice to know. I was embarrassed. But I needed her story. I thought something in it might save me.

Her bulbous lip perked up. "I wrote a note: 'I've saved my money, and now I'm gone. You'll never hit me again. No hard feelings. Goodbye.'"

I wanted to know which part made her smile, and if he drank, but my nerve failed me.

I spent my weekends driving to Detroit, stealing looks at him. I wondered if he shot up, in the basement, in cars, in the bars on the way home. I would never know, like I didn't know the other times. He didn't beat me. I didn't save up money. But day after day, I felt like those dried lawns burning up in the night.

Even though I never told her, Eunice must have smelled it on me— not the blaze but the sulfuric whiffs of a match just struck, the shadow of a man lurking in the dark, eyeing his chances.

"You have to be strong," she said. "That's what I learned."

I didn't know what strong meant, exactly.

"I wish I were mean," I said. "I've been reading about the Celtic pagan gods. Did you know there is no god of rain? It's Boann for rivers, Manannán mac Lir for sea and storms, and Bel for crops. Danu is the goddess of earth."

She sucked her teeth.

"But if you want a mean god, a get-even-Celtic-ballbuster, I'd go with Arwan, god of the underworld and revenge. Arwan would make sure your ex-husband never bothered you again."

"I'm not worried. He scared me at first. That's what he wanted. He was the rock, but my faith was the river." She nodded once, and smiled in a funny way. Not arrogant. Like a hen.

A few kids passed slowly, eyeing her house. They were fifteen at the most, smoking, glancing behind them. For a second, the kids looked as jaded as inmates. But the glances were false bravery, like the farmers who told me that any day now, rains would come.

"Eunice, I think your place is next."

So that night we tiptoed out in our bare feet. Eunice grabbed the garden hose, and when I turned the spigot, it ached with delight. Eunice smiled. "Jackson Prison, here we come."

When we watered the tinder patch at our feet, the grass melted and limped into the mud as if to say, "Oh, that feels good…right there." Step after step, we gave them to the glorious earth until they quivered with delight. We watered the entire postage stamp lawn this way until we felt our heels sink.

A dastardly smile erupted on Eunice's face. I should have known. She lifted the hose and sprayed me right in the face. I grabbed the hose back and managed to squirt part of her head. The meringue swirls went limp on the left side, as if her hair had had a stroke. We giggled like girls, feeling the moist, prickly grass wriggle to life under our wet toes. And who would stop us now?

When the cops passed, we hid behind the trees. When the kids came around again, they walked faster, as if they feared our wild power, as if we were fierce gods, the Arwans of Jackson, dancing in the summer of pyres.

# Bigfoot

IN THE COLD and snow, I told myself what moved in the woods was harmless. A moose, a stray dog. But then it shifted again, and I saw the yellow eyes, the shadow of a dog's body, but spindly and stalking. I'd taken the wrong turn, and now I was trying to trace my way back, following my lone footsteps, tracking myself to the beginning. The animal moved between pines. I should have picked cross-country skis instead of snow shoes. Going out on my own wasn't smart.

Paul and I broke up again, so I said yes to the first guy who asked me out. The athletic type. He moved in teams. Even this ski trip came with two friends who did Jägermeister shots on the way up. Once we pulled into Pine Knob, they had to ski The Wall. They all chanted, "Wall Wall Wall," and stomped their feet until the van shook.

When they finally stopped, I said, "Snowshoeing is more my style."

They eyed one another, and Carl shrugged. I left them to be alone, for something without the plunge. Snowshoes seemed affirming. You land with every step. I wanted to be out in nature, with the trees and birds. But once the cool, clean air hit me, a lingering hangover came to life. My head throbbed, my gut clenched. I stomped with my new, netted feet. It hurt to lift my legs. My organs barely chugged along. I had been hungover for some time, more weeks than days.

I would call Paul again, probably when I got home. But I had to change my life. This back and forth couldn't go on. This passed my mind when I saw the animal in a clearing. A coyote eyed me, a meal too big for him, unless I fell or hit my head, or maybe that was wrong. Maybe coyotes eat weak people, hungover people. Lost people.

I called up everything I knew about winter: snowflakes had six sides, hypothermia felt like beautiful sleep, and coyotes ate the small and the dead. Scavengers. The coyote's coat stood up in the back. I trudged along. Snowshoes weren't meant for running. I heaved my knees into my chest and lunged forward. My legs were heavy with the cold and the past. All around me nothing showed itself but this coyote and me. Maybe he was here to tell me I had taken the wrong turn. I was barely alive. Why did I go for the first guy who came along? I wanted distance. I wanted to throw it in Paul's face. What was I becoming? The wind had started to shift the snow over my tracks.

Close and far, it was only snow, but to the right, a thatch of tall pines braced together, their backs turned to the wind. I'd seen those trees earlier, so I made my way there.

Miles away, Carl glided down the mountain, *shoosh shoosh*. He drank all night, but was never hungover. He buried himself under piles of people and noise. Nothing stalked him; not regret, not woe. When we went out, we stayed up until 3 a.m. In the morning I would be sick. Carl would be bleary. "That was fun," he'd say. People spent entire lives this way, I thought, between parties.

The wind came bitter then. I would be sick—the gin sick of old ladies in pink fuzzy bathrobes. I clopped along, Bigfoot without the mystery. I didn't look back. One edge of the snowshoe slapped on the upward tip of the other, and I fell face-first into the snowy turf. My face there, in the melting, was all I had. I was a person who looked for the easy way out. I was a person who wanted to get even. I was a person who fell into the cold. I was someone predators saw as easy prey.

The guidebook said never play dead, so I acted like I was living. I got up and clomped. I was seven feet tall. I threw my arms into the air. I was a warrior. I was a tree: huge and mighty.

I touched one tree, then headed to one far away, hoping to throw the coyote off. I saw this bare, huge oak, with the leaves still on, dry as chimes in the air. It was one of those trees with the limbs so big they grew along the ground. How did it ever survive? I wrapped my arms around the tree and told myself it was just the hangover playing tricks. Paul was gone. I had lost my pack. I was far from home. There would be no next guy. I didn't want anyone else. My cries echoed through the deadness of winter. For a moment, I was tremendously, heart-wrenchingly enormous. I clung to this tree. The brittle oak leaves clinked in the wind. Then I left it and headed to what I hoped was the way out. My legs burned. I said things.

"I won't look back. The ground is not melting. I am big. I am not lost. That sound is not howling. I am big."

# Rise

THEY SAY THE men still stand at the corner of Cass and Temple in Detroit with their arms open wide and their bodies leaning against the wall like doors without houses.

They say we are all betrayal and laughter, and whose fault is it that the men have slid between these extremes, like the gravelly slits between buildings? The man with one leg still leans against the laundromat wall and looks out for the squeamish, who are fresh from expensive jobs and cheap bars. They slow down two blocks away, changing their minds. They say go back to your wife and forget all this. But one-legged dealers know there is no such thing as ambivalence here, only frequencies of need—that and the hard setting sun that has left everyone to the gray concrete. In such a place and such a time, it is easy to believe the only salvageable gesture is not turning away from a man who walks with a crutch and eats with his eyes.

They say the two vehicles are still parked there: a yellow Cadillac and a gray van with two windows in back. In the winter, when it is too cold to stand, the cars fill up with the men. The windows fog with breath and cigarette smoke. When the temperature hovers around zero, the Cadillac is so loaded that the muffler rests on the street like an anchor.

Nothing has changed as much for them as the things that have been left alone: the laundromat got fleas, then lost customers, and then died. The owner sits on the property and awaits the revolution, where souls might not be saved but you can sell high. The windows were punched out, and after a knife fight inside, the owner boarded up the place with plywood to avoid lawsuits and culpability. The top floor of the apartment building across the street caught fire last month. Now it hangs over the neighborhood like a paralyzed limb.

The women are different, of course, but they fizzle out the same way, like a sparkling drink that has sat too long on the bar. One of the guys was busted down on Willis and is serving six months, but whose fault is that, seeing as he worked outside the pack? So the group thins out a little. But the loss is temporary. He'll be back. Because in the end, it is not the events that change—the new people or the new buildings or the death—it is more the dull-witted sameness that consistently changes texture on its own.

They say you still go there. Even after the promises and people who tried to help you, and the money, you go back. Eventually, you drive by just to check the place out, and, well, you know the rest. They see you coming a block away. They recognize the car. The short guy is in the middle of a story, but he catches sight and waves then nudges the guy with one leg, and he waves. Pretty soon all the guys are turning around and waiting for you to stop. You tell yourself it is the kindness in you: to see the worth in people when others may not. But you know it is not decency that makes you stop. You've said before where the urge comes from: a junkie is always a narcissist. People make such desires romantic and grandiose. People trapped, and people in war. But you know it is a headache like any habit is a headache. It is domestic and boring and chains you to the hours like a wooden bird in an old German clock who must crawl out on the ledge every sixty minutes and peep.

They tell me for protection, to save me from the surprise of seeing you stumble through the view of something else. But wounds heal, and every prisoner in Jackson is innocent. Just ask them. The robbery we thought was leveled upon us—the stealing of money and mothers and fairness—we created ourselves by believing life did not give us everything that mattered. The slander we gave the sky, the stars cried back to us, so unhappy, so bent by loving what could not love alone.

This is where I should pull out a pretty metaphor, something from nature about me having forgiven you. But all I have left in my bag of tricks is some magic corn and a past I can feel but can't touch. And I don't realize it until I drive to the pumpkin sale over by Trumbull and see the most beautiful man in red overalls and a paper hat carrying his two pumpkins through the emerald grass. The leaves fall in the sun, and a little girl's mother has bundled her up like a Weeble. The girl throws her stuffed arms out and yells, "Yay!" as if the trees are throwing confetti.

Then I see there is no more of us here. The days run so fast together that they collapse on their own. It aches sometimes to see them go, to see what I am and what I still yearn to be. They never told me about this strange vibration, what it is to be happy. It hurts at first when the lock we once called "fate" snaps by choice. I do not know it until I park at the pumpkin sale and walk into the studio. The pumpkins sit out like guests, round wallflowers waiting to be asked for the next dance. Then, after years, even though I tried to forget it all, finally, my dear, I do not travel down those roads anymore. And if you were to arrive in any of these scenes, the moment wouldn't know what to do with you. Another door without a home. Another hope that ended up in my pile of "too bads."

Give all the men down at the corner blades to hack away the loneliness. But for the women like me, reserve memory, since she'll slice the beating heart from the wreckage. She'll crack it all on a whisper. Ashes to ashes. Dust to dust. Let me live again.

# The Ways of Accidents

"THERE'S A BODY but no blood, and he doesn't even look dead," Bill says, "so why not come on down and get your jollies?"

I know what the recovery books say: avoid stress, focus on sobriety, get rest, and exercise. But the adrenaline kicks in. I have a 9 a.m. deadline. I have to give it everything this time. I have to do it right.

It's 5 a.m. I grab my reporter's notebook, mark day fourteen on the calendar, and fishtail it up Westnedge Hill. By 5:10 a.m., I'm coasting down into the dark, icy ass of morning.

An Alberta Clipper raced in last night. The rain turned to ice, which falls on the snow like glass beads. The only way to tell the street from the curb is a stoplight ahead, which I glide under, red, yellow, green—whatever. I couldn't brake if I wanted to. The pellets ping off the windshield, and I skim around the corner with the Taco Bell and out past where the pharmaceutical company shut down.

All the buildings are flat. You can't miss the site for the squad cars with the whirling lights that flash above the industrial warehouses and against the dark sky.

I turn the steering wheel right, but the car drives straight. I tap the brake, back up, and inch my way to the barricade, which is just some rookies, Thompson and Balis, with their palms open and not enough sense to move clear from the path of my bald tires. It's 5:30 a.m.

I roll down the window. When Thompson leans his arms on my door, his leather squeaks and aches.

"Hear you've got a body," I say.

"You got any press credentials?"

"Drop dead, Thompson."

Balis, arms akimbo, walks into my headlights, kicks the fender as if he's about to buy the thing, and saunters over to Thompson. "Disrespecting an officer?" He lifts up on the balls of his feet, sniffs, and hoists his belt. "I believe that's an incarcerable offense."

"Incarcerable?" Thompson turns to him. "Honestly, Balis, where do you get this stuff?" He stands back and waves me through.

The thin layer of ice crunches under my tires as I pass the flat, brick building to my right and inch toward the somber ricochet of red and blue police lights. I make a mental note to get the company name.

In the back parking lot, Bill stands between the scene and the high beams of his squad car, his thin, 6'5" frame casting a shadow against the body.

I don't want to look, but I know in a flash that it's bad. The victim is lifted up a foot or two in the air, pinned at an angle between a wrecker and a metal waste bin. Cords are involved. His head is tilted toward us, he faces forward, his mouth agape. The bin is full of junk. The back has wheels. Yellow caution tape surrounds the scene.

Bill narrows in on the rookies. "You two ladies planning on working today or do you want to finish your tea first?"

Bill's height, nearly a foot taller than my own, does not intimidate me, nor does his gnarly expression, which he has honed over the years. Balis and Thompson hustle to the scene.

Maybe it's the night or my situation, but I've covered a lot of fatalities on this job and in each I see one of three stages. In stage one, the being of the person stays in the body, as if letting go would plunge them into Dante's Inferno. In the second, the soul hangs around hoping for something. I covered a death on Portage Road, for example, when a semi hit a Festiva, killing the driver. Her energy hovered nearby, hoping for answers, or family. I could see her body, but also felt her at my back, whispering, "Tell them I'm here." The family did come, and the woman's energy lingered there, then passed on to stage three, when the deceased finally accepts her fate and abandons the body like a gum wrapper.

This guy is stage two, the waiting. I have known Bill, a lieutenant, for four years and have never mentioned this. He'll think I'm mental or use it as further proof.

"So, what do we have here?" I ask stupidly.

Bill looks down at me with his owl eyes. A strip of white hair runs from one ear to the next. "Well, Sherlock…"

"Don't do that," I say.

"What?"

"That's such a cop thing to say."

Bill doesn't yell at me. He teases me, sure, but even if I snap at him, he brushes it off like the ice pellets on his hat. I don't know how I warrant this status, because he yells at everyone else.

Deep down, I think he knows I quit drinking, and I quit in a way he could respect. No rehab and no therapy. Cold turkey. I don't know if I need to quit drinking forever, but the threat of job termination seems as good a reason as any to stop for a while.

I come from a family of coal miners and government workers. We don't get fired, and we certainly don't get fired for booze. A working man, or woman, has the balls to drink herself under the table and get up to put in a full day. Besides, Detroiters don't get hangovers. They have headaches. They have cranky, insolent attitudes. Hangovers are for preppies and wimps. Even if I've moved to Kalamazoo for this job, I still hold myself to these cultural standards.

With little else to observe or write down, I look at the accident for the first time. The guy's back is pressed against the front of the bin. The taut cord descends from the truck pulley, under his left arm, across his chest, and down below the bin. He hangs there, icicles on the end of his glasses, feet suspended in the air. He wears tan coveralls, the kind that zip up the front. He has an urgent expression on his face. His mouth makes an "O" in a way that asks you to finish the word for him.

Bill turns to look at me. "You okay?"

"Don't worry about me. I'm a survivor."

"The fact you think you're a survivor is what worries me."

Quitting drinking means turning up the stereo on your life. Your problems are louder, with deep bass notes. The bodies, for example, are too much. The freak accidents are the worst. You can look at a body and see an essential unfairness in the world, where even final thoughts are cut short.

I wonder if Bill quit drinking, because his stereo is on blast. Last week he told a sergeant to go fuck himself. Bill's always being written up or reprimanded, which is why I see him so often in the odd hours: nights, weekends, and holidays. It's like he's on perpetual punishment.

Consequently, Bill and I meet at the violent deaths, since those always happen at night; and a surprising majority in the winter. In four years, we've seen one murder, six car crash fatalities, and four shootings, including two domestics.

Bill's breath plumes in a way that reminds me of a bull in the field.

I look down at my black suede boots with the pointy heel. "Do we have any witnesses?"

"His last work contact appears to be 6:40 p.m. yesterday," Bill says.

"Name?"

"Fergus."

My pen freezes, and I shake it.

Bill pulls a felt-tip out of his chest pocket. "Didn't they teach you anything in school?"

I look up, and the ice falls on my face. I can't help looking at the crystals' sparkle and fortitude. "I guess not."

"Fergus Plowman, conventional spelling."

I spell out the letters anyway, just to be sure. Bill studies his men and tries hard not to be funny. "Now let's see if those brainiacs down at the paper screw it up."

He walks under the yellow tape, then turns and lifts it for me. "Come on."

"I'm good here."

"You have to know what happened, don't you? Isn't that why you came here?"

I slip under the yellow line and write down everything I can: Red Wing boots, John Denver glasses, gray hair, short, bare hands; wedding ring.

"Time of death?"

"Undetermined."

"Given his condition…"

"Fergus is a human popsicle," Balis says.

"Balis, do your job and cut the crap. This is your last warning." Bill turns to me. "And his work schedule, we're estimating the time of the accident as after 7 p.m. and before midnight."

"This was probably his last haul," I say. "He was in a hurry."

Bill nods. "Possibly."

Bill's received plenty of service medals, and he has over twenty-five years in the department, so I don't understand the anger. He could ride it out, retire in seven if he kept his mouth shut. But that's increasingly hard to do.

"You're stressing yourself out with all of this anger," I told him once.

"Well you need a little bit more anger," Bill responded.

Bill thinks I should tell my bosses to go get bent, drop dead, or any of the other special phrases he's mastered over the years. But he doesn't understand.

Bill, in fact, should worry. "I'm afraid they'll fire you," I say.

The ice sparkles in the distance like a sugar coat.

He looks down at me, straining to be patient. "Sometimes, Mary, your dignity is more important than some frigging job."

This is what Bill knows: a couple months ago, at 3 a.m., I showed up at a fatality down on County Line Road. It was an ugly scene: cars smashed, glass and blood everywhere, a body, an actual person, still slumped over the steering wheel.

I ran to the side of the road and puked. When I returned, Bill handed me some Kleenex. "It's a bad scene, kid. I don't blame you. I puked the first time I saw a body."

Bill seemed to forget it wasn't my first time. And Bill didn't know that I was hungover. I'd bought vodka the night before, which was a big mistake. You can't really taste it in juice. And before you know it, you can barely stand up. I started thinking about the guy I met in Kalamazoo, John, who had just accepted a job in Minneapolis. He wanted me to go, too. I couldn't blame him. But I wanted to say, "Don't go." He seemed choked up about it. But you can't hold people back, especially when you're barely holding on yourself. I kept my mouth shut.

Since I quit drinking, my mornings are free of headaches, sour stomachs, and, most times, shame. But at night the cravings come. The drive home from work is the worst. I think about my unhappy editors, and then all I see are the bodies, or the dope dealers, or the mistakes I made in writing stories, or where John is now, and all of those worries swirl around until I find myself at home, with bottles of wine, not sure how they got there.

Every evening I fight these urges, just so I can feel some shred of pride in the morning: eleven days, twelve days, thirteen days, and not one drink. I repeated these facts on the way home last night. It's my version of the personal headlines. Mary did not drink today. She held her ground. In an epic fit of heroism, Mary drove straight home.

After I got sick at the County Line Road accident, I couldn't stop staring at the scene, the blood, the lifelessness, the hovering spirit, waiting for someone.

Bill reconstructed the accident, the sixteen-year-olds, the running of a red light, the impact. Maybe it was the nausea, but I felt the girl's presence near me: "Get my mom. Tell her I'm so sorry." I kept wondering if it had to be this way, her entire life changing direction because she blew through a red light. I could feel this kid's life hanging out, seeing herself in the car, not sure what happened, because this could not be happening.

"Same old story, right, Bill?"

He nodded. "Same dumb kids, different day."

I went back to the office and wrote up the story before heading off to a pot bust. The editors heard about the puking incident from the photographer. It didn't take a brain surgeon to stitch it all together: my bleary morning eyes, my vague sentences, my puking. They couldn't prove it, of course, but one editor called me unprofessional and wrote me up.

When I called my sister Meghan, the art therapist, and told her about puking at the fatality, she seemed more alarmed at my indifference. I told her facts of my drinking without insight or understanding. All I felt was shame. I threw in my philosophy of the three stages just to change the subject. Meghan saw right through me.

"You know what you just saw?"

"What?"

"Your shadow. Your three-stages theory? Well, you are in stage one. Denial. You're not a careless teenager. Your man leaves town and you hate your job. If you don't start listening, some big shit is going to hit you in the face."

"Thanks for the pep talk."

"You didn't call me for a pep talk. Quit drinking. Start painting."

I wasn't the worst drinker in the world. Far from it. Mostly I stuck to wine, so it surprised me that I had trouble quitting. Eventually, I changed my route, ate something standing in front of the fridge, then got in bed and read books as though I was sick. In bed, I didn't want wine. I wanted John to call.

In journalism, you can't write what you can't prove, which is everything. I can't write, for example, that notifying the Plowman family is far worse than actually seeing Fergus.

"Why not let Balis call the family?" I ask.

"That's my job," Bill says. "Besides, it's done."

"It's done?"

He nods and swipes the ice off his hat.

At most fatalities, someone is usually there to help. It's beautiful when you think about it. Mothers comfort, EMS techs administer CPR, and strangers get out of their cars.

I'm there to get the facts right, to help people who know the deceased, or help right an injustice. When I call the families, I just listen to the weeping, wailing parents trying to choke through something about the deceased for the morning edition. Of course, it's heartbreaking. I can't write about that, either.

"Come on, Einsteins," Bill says to the rookies. "Let's get this show on the road. What have we got?"

"We've got a fifty-five-year-old white male truck driver alone," Thompson says.

"How do we know that, Balis?" Bill asks.

"No other footprints," Balis says. "No other tracks."

"Come again?"

"No obvious tire or foot tracks, sir."

"The cause of the accident, Thompson?"

Balis shakes his head. "Where do you start?"

Thompson says, "There appears to be weather-related issues. The wrecker is up against the bin, which is too close, and the wrecker cable is across his chest here."

Thompson runs his finger across the line, now caked with ice. "My guess is the cable had a lot of slack when it froze or malfunctioned. Mr. Plowman went back to investigate. He probably pulled the cable, then the slack released, and the bin, with Mr. Plowman's back pressed against it, lifted up."

"Huh," Balis says.

It is an amazing assessment, one I hadn't considered.

"Why are his feet and arms out?" I ask.

Bill shrugs. "Maybe impact, or a struggle."

We stand there.

Finally Bill pulls at the frozen cable. "Expect a call from OSHA. This is the wrong truck for the job."

Bill takes a pen and tracks the cable from the truck to the bin lift, and down across Fergus's chest. Bill keeps stabbing, ice flying everywhere, until he sees what he's looking for. "Uh huh."

"The truck was too close, otherwise he might have lived with a broken arm."

We stand there, trying to measure the odds.

"It was probably the last haul of the night. How do we know that, Thompson?"

"Work would have questioned when he failed to appear at other jobs," Thompson says. "Someone would have checked, sir."

"We have a call in to the company," Balis says, "to verify the victim's assigned location, job, and the approximate time of his work here."

"Good," Bill says. "So what factors caused this accident?"

"Faulty equipment and the storm. Also, Mr. Plowman appeared to be without a hat and gloves. Notice the burn marks across his hands,"

Thompson says. "The temperature could have been a factor in his reasoning skills. Mr. Plowman appears to have been working alone without the ability to call for assistance."

"His death appears instantaneous. Be sure to get that in," Bill says in a soft, thankful tone.

I look at Fergus, up close; really look at him. He doesn't look dead. All the evidence is there. Icicles dangle from his glasses. His eyes are frozen open, his jaw drops in a way we blame on gravity. He has stubble on his chin.

No one really talks around bodies, and I know why after covering so many deaths. Thoughts turn strange around them. With the body and the cold, I think there is nothing wrong with Fergus that a match and a good Sterno can't fix.

I wiggle one boot, then the other.

"You feel like dancing?" Bill asks.

"My feet have gone numb."

"Well what the hell are you wearing those dainty things for? You got a date after this or something?"

I look down at my boots with the little heel and the suede, wet and ruined. "I guess I'm vain."

Bill answers a page on the walkie-talkie. "They're on their way."

"Who's on their way?" I ask.

Thompson gets a blanket and a lock cutter from his trunk. He lays it out on the ground. "The family. They're driving out from Chelsea."

"Bill, didn't you call the EMS?"

This is procedure. You must ensure no possibility of revival and confirm the time of death. Plus, they take the body.

"The family has requested to see Mr. Plowman alone."

Bill joins Thompson, Balis, and the other officers in a semicircle around Mr. Plowman. Thompson uses the lock cutter to cut the cable. They all crouch down and hold their arms out, in case the body falls forward. Fergus stays frozen to the truck.

"He's not moving," Balis says.

Thompson looks at Balis. "You're just figuring that out?"

Thompson and Balis walk up and yank Fergus out like a tooth. They place him on a blanket, flat on his back, but his arms and knees are frozen up in the air. We stare at Mr. Plowman, chiseled, with his bent knees, his arms stretching outward. His whole body seems to be reaching for something, for someone. And for some reason, the stages don't fit now. It is a mixture of too many emotions, too much sadness to divide.

I say whatever comes out of my mouth to break the silence. "He made a mistake."

"There are no mistakes," Bill says. "No mistakes and no accidents."

I study his face to see if this is a joke. "You think there's a reason for everything?"

"Sure."

I wipe my nose. "That's kind of stressful."

"Better than no reason at all."

"I don't know, Bill," I say. "I'm pro-ambiguity."

"I bet Fergus was chock-full of doubts, too. Now look at him."

"Ambiguity and doubts are two different things."

"Tell that to Fergus. It's all happening for a reason. See the signs."

Bill turns to his men. "Throw a blanket over the guy. Let's get him thawed out before the family comes. He looks like Jesus in the crib, for Christ's sake."

The guys turn with slow surprise from Bill to the body. Bill's right. We wait for something, anything, to reveal itself.

Balis sneezes.

"Balis is getting a coldy-woldy," Thompson says. "Maybe we should call his mommy."

Balis sneezes again. Then he and Thompson walk to their squad car out by the road to get more blankets.

"Bill," I whisper.

"Look, kid, they're driving here through this storm, against my advisement, to see where he died. They have asked this one thing."

My breath fogs in the air. A truck passes out front. Now I can feel Fergus there, hovering.

"You fear nothing," I say. "Maybe that's a bad thing."

Bill stares out into the distance, conjuring a memory. "The fear of death follows from the fear of life. A man who lives fully is prepared to die at any time." He sniffs. "Mark Twain."

This quote shakes me to the core, worse than the cold. I can't let him see that, though. "Well played," I say.

Bill saunters over to check the truck for anything out of the ordinary: firearms, alcohol, drugs, or paraphernalia. He looks in the cab, checks the glove box, and runs his hands around and behind the seat. He reaches under the driver's seat. He pulls something out slowly, like he's afraid to see the outcome. In Bill's hand is a fifth of Smirnoff. It's half empty.

The ice bounces off us. We stare at the thing. Nobody has seen anything.

You can get stuck in a life. That's what I see now. But when you're in that life you can't see it, because you are in the darkness, and it's cold and lonely. You think it can never get better. That's the real addiction. You go on, because you believe this is all there is. I understand Mr. Plowman. The shame, the regret, the deadness inside. He's here. I can feel his presence. *Don't let me die a mistake.*

The family is on their way. That bottle could have been there a long time.

I've never done anything like this before. But I lean over and nudge Bill. "Let's spare them," I say. I open my purse. Without hesitation, he drops the fifth into it. I zip up my purse. I sniff and sense relief in the air, an expunging of anguish.

Bill points his finger at me. "I trust you. Don't screw this up."

A faint line of light runs along the eastern buildings. Something comes to me as a surprise. "Bill, on this, I won't let you down."

We look over to Mr. Plowman, who, with every speck of ice, is already being claimed by the earth.

No one moves. Not for a long time.

Fergus reaches out to the world, and it walks closer to him, in collusion.

"I guess it's wrong to make a metaphor of the dead."

Bill pats my back. "Somehow, Mary, I think Fergus would be okay with that."

Bill turns to the other officers. "Are you knitting that blanket, or what? Get the thing on him already."

Thompson opens the first blanket and throws it over Fergus's feet. Balis carefully places his over the torso. Bill whips his blanket in the air in a way that looks like a raven flying free. Then the thing opens up, and Bill lowers the fluttering fabric over Fergus's head.

Bill stands over the woolly mound and closes his eyes. I think he is saying a prayer. Balis looks at Bill with the expression people use when they watch ice skaters fall. Bill doesn't care. I bow my head with him and say my own prayer.

I open my eyes. "I think I'm going to take off."

Bill waits until I've started to walk away, then says, "So long, toots."

Something in his voice makes me turn back. "So long, Bill." I smile. Then I know what will happen before it is done.

Bill turns back, cool air billowing out of his nostrils.

I get in my car.

The roads are more slippery than when I arrived. I grip the steering wheel and creep along. I'll go in to work, write up the story, take what I need, and walk out that door for good. Meghan was right. I drank for reasons. I hate my job and miss John. These are the facts. If you want to live, the first step is to respect how the facts reveal patterns, to abide by the ways of accidents.

As I drive to my last day of work, I picture Bill at the scene, opening the car door for that wife and those daughters, explaining patiently how the incident occurred. This much Bill will give them.

He tells them that when they found Fergus, he seemed to be calling out to someone, probably for them.

Bill nods firmly, his eyes steely behind his visor. "Without a doubt."

Bill stands there as long as they need, until the weight of loss falls all around them like ice.

On the road, I remember something. I unzip my purse, open my window, and pitch the Smirnoff out into the snow.

The dawn will come, but for a moment, it's still dark. Ice pellets fly off my windshield.

It's all right. I know my way by the stoplight ahead. Red, yellow, green. It doesn't matter.

It just takes one light beaming out of the darkness to get you there.

# Tainted

ON THE FIRST day of jury duty at the Hennepin County Government Center, I sat in the crammed room and eyed the men wearing hunting caps. A woman clacked her knitting needles. Despite the lack of metal detectors, I told myself people wouldn't dare bring guns. I gripped my bike helmet and waited.

A court employee lectured the packed room about the indecency of chewing gum, reading, and talking while in the presence of a judge. A woman from the jury pool yelled out: "I have kids and no sitter, for crying out loud."

"I have kids, too," another woman shouted.

A man stood up. "I'll lose my job if I'm called."

Try as I might to maintain my composure, hope flooded my heart. The crowd could murder the court employee—shoot him, tear him limb from limb. Those not charged with murder would be tainted and sent home.

I told myself this was the sort of thinking that needed correction. I had been called, and it was my duty to serve.

The employee lectured (while rocking from his heels to his tiptoes) that those with special circumstances could line up and proclaim their plight to the court administrator, who worked out of the office to the right, and would arrive at any minute. Potential jurors heaved themselves at the door. The remaining people sat quietly, stewing in their lack of creativity.

After the lecture, I took my purse and bike helmet and found an empty seat in a nearby jury box. I put my feet up on the faux wood banister and tried unsuccessfully to read my book, *The Trial*, which seemed like a good choice at home but now only mirrored the room. Out of five people called, three sighed as they stood up.

Someone had left newspapers. I read the "Life" section. I studied the brown, 1970s plywood, the dull caramel carpeting, and the indifferent walls.

The second day passed. People were called into juries, others got out. One man said to a woman, "He should have gotten off."

"Excuse me," I said to a woman reading a romance novel. "Do you think many people are dismissed from these jury duties?"

"Some, sure," the woman said. She was kind and solid, like mortar. "But they go fast. I just finished one, and if I get one more, I go home."

"Do you like that book?"

She glanced at the cover. "Yes. I like the writer. Kind of addictive."

I nodded. "That's nice."

On the third day, I was called. The defendant, a young man, a child really, sat in an oversized suit coat. The judge explained the case: the man (child) was accused of fatally shooting another man.

The judge explained it was a murder trial. The defendant's head was on the table, as though he was asleep.

My first instinct was to try and stop this nightmare. Punch myself, maybe. I could put on the helmet and say, "Doctor's orders."

But I corrected myself. These ideas were irrational, even cruel. One had to accept her situation. As a member of the jury, maybe I could see the truth of the situation, maybe my experience would offer unique insights.

The judge asked people about their professions. One woman said, "I'm a lawyer." She was kicked off right away.

The judge turned and looked at me, "What do you do for a living?"

"Teacher," I said. The judge nodded. The lawyers studied their paperwork and whispered to one another.

I sat in the front row. The judge proceeded with general questions for the group. Had anyone on the jury ever been robbed? I raised my hand.

"Anyone ever had trouble with a drug dealer?" I raised my hand.

"Anyone ever have trouble with a police officer?"

Up went my hand. Of course, I thought. Hasn't everyone?

"Known an addict?"

Please, I thought, my hand raised again. This was America. Who doesn't know an addict but the addict himself?

"How many times have you been robbed?" the judge asked. It took a second to realize he was asking me. My eyes narrowed in thought.

"Well, four, I think, no...wait. Five."

The judge laced his fingers and leaned forward. "You're not sure?"

It was complicated. I explained the first time when the guy broke into my parents' house and the dog bit him, so he ran away. The next day the lawnmower was gone from the garage. The second and third times were attempts, which didn't count, but they got in the house, and my father screamed, "Hey, we called the cops!" or the dog chased him away. Then in high school, some guy pulled a backpack right off me in the middle of the day and just walked off. He didn't even bother to run, because he knew a girl couldn't do anything anyway. Then in college, someone broke into my apartment when I was asleep and stole everything, which, in retrospect, looked like a setup, where a guy at a bar had drugged me, but that was a guess. I never found out for sure. Then there were the multiple car break-ins, and a friend murdered by the Oakland County Killer, which was the biggest theft—the theft of life—a girl stolen from her childhood; and, of course, there were the drug dealers who lived next door, so famous they ended up in a book, because the main guy sold the biggest amount of heroin ever to an undercover DEA agent. And then there was the cop who used to find me and my friend at the park and give us flowers, which was weird. We heard later that he walked a girl to her door, and when she turned around to thank him, his dick was hanging out of his pants. So those stories were thefts, too, thefts of humanity, of decency. Then I realized I was rambling, and not internally. I was talking out loud to the judge, to strangers.

119

I paused and said, "So, you know, the typical stuff."

The judge sat back. "Do you think these experiences will influence your judgment on this jury?"

How does someone answer that question? I didn't know. I checked the stove and door three times before I left. I always look around before exiting and entering a vehicle.

"I've learned a lot."

"Like what?"

"Well, I used to always carry keys between my fingers, so if I was attacked, I could stab the guy in the eyes. But now I've learned it's best to make a swift punch to the neck."

I had other tips, but chief among them was how to read a room. This one had gone quiet.

"The neck is sensitive," I said.

Still quiet.

"And it's more efficient," I said. "Besides, who has the guts to take out an eye?"

The judge said he needed a break. While we waited, a guy next to me said, "Isn't this exciting?"

The judge returned and said to me, "Both sides have agreed to let you go."

I couldn't hear what the judge said after that, something about being sorry for those times.

The accused and the sheriff watched me leave.

Outside, I walked right up to where I'd locked my bicycle. There was the bike post, but there was no bike. I stood there with a stare meant to bring the bike into view. I thought maybe I'd locked it in a different spot, so I walked around the dark hull where the building hung over the street and then asked the security guard on duty, who walked with me and showed me how the expensive bikes had two locks, one horseshoe and one wire.

My bike model had been discontinued. It was red and smart, like the tricycle I had as a child. When I rode it around downtown, people admired its curvy frame.

But now, well, "Is there a chance you locked it someplace else and forgot? Sometimes that happens."

"Yes," I said. I held my bike helmet as we walked around one corner, looking across the road to the signposts where other bikes were locked.

"Nothing there," the guard said, and then we turned a corner, and another, until we were not looking anymore but simply walking around the block.

The guard offered a global perspective. "This happens all the time. You can buy the most expensive lock in the world, but if someone really wants your bike, they'll find a way to get it."

I thought back to the judge's original question. "These experiences have influenced me," I said.

The guard didn't know what to make of such a comment. "Hey, don't blame yourself," he said finally.

I stared at his kind face. "Okay." I thanked him and left.

I walked home under a bold, wide sky. I was tired of holding the helmet, so I put it on. I snapped the buckle closed. A man walking by veered away from me. A woman did the same, then another, with a look of fear, then compassion.

I passed the buildings, the slowing cars. I saw the concern of passersby. I wanted to console them. "It's okay. It feels good. It's like an extra brain." Instead, I thought of the boy asleep, my bike moving on without me, and the defendant who didn't get off. I saw the objects and the people behind the objects and felt an opening, where something broke free across my sky. *My life, my life, you have not forsaken me.*

# Squeak

ONE NIGHT, WE decided to bury the rat. I'm still not sure how it all started. Mel had chosen her outfit, a black, velvet dress and spike-heeled boots. She had begun the long process of getting dressed, while Laura and I sat on the couch and sipped vodka gimlets, listening to a stuck car whir its wheels. It was the end of winter, when the season's snow compacted into ice, and any warmth created slick pools on the frozen surface. This simple fact of nature wreaked havoc in the streets, where cars slid together, and people walked in a perpetual state of almost falling. Since moving here, I still hadn't adjusted to the bitter winter, or the spring that came too late.

Today, all life felt slippery. Laura was explaining, for example, that she'd changed her mind about our plans. She did not, in fact, want us to meet her new boyfriend at a bar.

"M-m-m-maybe we should leave Tom at the Lex," Laura said. "Let him stew."

She flicked her cigarette and held her head high. Through half a year of speech therapy, Laura had resolved most of her stutter.

"Did he cheat on you?"

"No," Laura said, and turned away. Very dignified. Tactfully composed. Distant as a landscape.

It would take hours to mete out a few facts: Tom had said something rude; Laura, in response, had gotten drunk; Laura was a

123

little thing, so two drinks were one too many. "I didn't know I c-c-could drink six shots of tequila," Laura said. "Threw up in his car, too. S-s-serves him right."

Mel lived on the sixth floor, where the heat collected, so she'd opened the windows for air. The car wheels still spun in the alley and when we popped our heads out over the window ledge, we saw the front right tire had slipped into a pothole, and the remaining wheels rotated on a sort of soggy ice rink.

Mel walked in with her clicking heels and bright smile. "We could go there and ignore him. That'd be fun."

They'd just changed Mel's meds, and with her strawberry blonde hair and makeup, she looked like a movie star in the middle of a happy ending.

"What'd you do with your old meds?" I asked.

Mel lit a cigarette and asked, "Why?"

She'd stopped the last pills because they raised her voice two octaves and made her "super-duper happy." She said she felt like an airplane revving up for a crash. She lost a little weight. Just the sort of supplement I was looking for.

"Can I have them?" I ask.

I wasn't ill. I just needed a tool for transitioning. The move to Minnesota had been more stressful than I had anticipated. I just needed something for the adjustment. A little weed, a drop of acid, or some mushrooms would take care of it. But I didn't know anyone here with that sort of remedy. I'd pop an anti-anxiety pill in a pinch, as long as I wasn't permanently medicated. Other people could do what they wanted for what ailed them, but I'd seen prescription drugs kill people quicker than heroin, and, at the risk of sounding practical, pharmaceuticals were expensive.

"I don't know," Mel said.

If I found them, she'd let me have a sample.

"Be right back," I said. In the bathroom, I searched the medicine cabinet, found nothing, and felt guilty.

I heard them talking in the kitchen. I walked in just as Laura was saying, "I have too much self-respect for this."

Mel nodded.

"For what?" I asked.

"You know," Laura said, then trailed off.

I checked the fridge, then opened the freezer. Maybe she liked to keep pills frozen, like vodka, or ice cream. I found nothing but two empty ice trays, and a plastic baggie. I thought, at first, that the baggie contained a moldy chicken breast. But it had feet and frost collected along its thin, pink tail. The animal had coarse and short hair, and paper-thin lids covered the eyes. The front feet or paws or whatever you call them resembled miniature hands, curled under its chin.

Mel was pouring a drink.

"Mel, you ever bury Squeak?"

"Yeah," she said.

I walked up behind Laura and put the bag in Mel's face.

"So, what's this?" I asked.

Laura screamed and ran to the other side of the room. "Jesus."

Mel rolled her eyes. "It's winter, okay? You can't get below snow in winter."

I felt bad for Mel, and Squeak. Animals should go to the ground, and she knew it, too. Normally, I would put the rat back in the freezer and forget about it. But that felt like suppression, which was dangerous. Squeak deserved better.

"Well, it's not winter, anymore," I said. "We should bury her now."

In Detroit, Chicago, or Toledo, this was winter. But in the northern Midwest, where you felt as though you walked on the earth's shoulders, thirty-five degrees was happy news.

"God, don't open it, you could set off the bubonic plague or something," Laura said. "Mel, it's not sanitary."

Mel looked down on the floor and said, "Yeah, maybe we could have a little ceremony."

I knew what she was thinking. Mel didn't want to bury Squeak. After the death of her brother, Mel bought Squeak at the pet store. Whenever we talked on the phone, Mel was always giggling at something Squeak did. Squeak poked her nose at the television and scampered around the painted furniture like she was having a rat emergency.

"This is all a little fast, isn't it?" Mel said. She petted Squeak through the plastic. Did I, in my sudden wisdom, recognize the projection of my woes into a single act meant to solve someone else's problems? Yes. Did I care? Yes. Did that stop me? Since when did that stop anyone?

We put our coats on, walked down three flights of stairs, and knocked on the super's door. He yelled "What?" and Mel said, "I need a shovel, Bert."

Bert opened the door and pointed to the snow shovel in the hall and Mel said, "No the burying kind." From the hallway you could see that Bert liked blue, on his walls, on his shirt. Someone moved in the apartment. For some reason, that made all of us stiffen. Bert kept to himself, and because of this, we knew all sorts of details about him, things Mel heard from the neighbors: he moved slow because of a neurological disorder, and he had watched *Dirty Harry* a hundred times. Bert was also a Camus freak, and any question might lead to a lecture about Camus' opaque optimism, with quotes that had become clichés: "In the depth of winter I finally learned that there was in me an invincible summer," and "The absurd is the essential concept and the first truth." It would be interesting if Bert didn't lecture for ten minutes, drawing out every word, and just when we thought he was done, he'd pick up another point. Add to this, we always had the suspicion that he was about to scratch his nuts from the outside of his blue jeans.

"Just a sec." Bert closed the door, and someone turned on the music to block any noise, which made us wonder what required noise. Mel lifted the bag to look at Squeak just as Bert, holding a shovel, opened the door. He stepped back when he saw the bag.

"What'd you go and do that for?"

"What?" Mel asked.

"If you got a rat problem, come to me," Bert said. He stopped there for a second, as if this might be his complete thought. We didn't know what to do. "Don't be clubbing them yourself. It makes me look bad."

"No, you don't—" and Mel meant to say *understand*, but Bert gently swung the door with one hand, and we all watched him look blankly from the other side as the door closed so slowly it barely registered a final click.

Mel gave me the shovel. "It was your idea."

"Of course," I said. "I would be honored."

Outside, the wheels whirred on and police car lights ricocheted through the street. A wrecker arrived and backed into the alley, the shrill reverse warning beeps pinging against the apartment walls. We slid along the sidewalk, like an ice tray left out all morning. Laura and I had to hold on to one another for balance. Mel's boots spiked through the icy surface. The snowbanks, heavy and disillusioned, receded in the center, but rimmed the park like a soggy scarf. Grass poked out here and there. Laura kept her eyes to the ground. She said every spring you could find what others had lost all winter. She spread her hands over the mud and got up, then walked away from us. In the distance she resembled a landmine expert sent ahead of the pack. As I walked, I pounded the shovel into the ground. Its blade head hit with a satisfying slice.

Passing cars showed the wounds of a hard winter, with rust, doused headlights, wheezing engines and whining, exhausted belts. They clunked into potholes with slightly deflated tires and, chalky with salt, passed like noisy ghosts under the streetlights. My car had broken down twice already, once on the freeway, and once right in front of my apartment, where the engine died, and I glided into a parking spot with amazing luck, since it was ten degrees below zero.

"Maybe it's still too early," Mel said.

She held the baggie up to her face. "I don't want her to melt if we can't hit through dirt."

Laura made her way back. The park, with the square corners of a city block, had trees to the east, and a small playground to the west. Mel pointed to the western end of the playground with the orange swing set. "She'd like it there."

Mel's heel sunk in a soft patch of mud, and when I went to help, the lift of my shoes made sucking noises.

The park was surrounded by lights from apartment windows—candles, lamps, and some with Christmas lights people couldn't bear to take down. Television screens spasmed with color. Whenever I saw those reflections in the night, I wanted to yell, "No, don't waste your life." But who was I to judge?

"By the swing," Mel said, "so she can watch the children play."

I felt Mel's sadness.

"We don't have to, Mel," I said. "We can do it another night."

She shrugged her shoulders and winced. "Let's see what happens."

Laura folded her arms and had a look of regret.

I said, "Tom is probably still waiting at the bar. Should we call him?"

Laura said slowly, determined not to stutter. "We met his old girlfriend at a party. The way he looked at her, I knew it all. Tom introduced me as his friend. His *friend*. Tom had told me that he dumped her. She was cold, he said. But it was a lie. I knew it then. She'd dumped him."

"Shit," I said.

"I'm no one's runner-up," she said.

Maybe Laura and I both needed a way to ease the edge.

"Mel, how about those extra pills," I said. "Help me out."

John reassured me it was tough for him, too. He'd moved here six months before me. I'd adjust. But it didn't feel right. I missed my friends, the steam pluming through the manholes on Second Avenue, the late nights watching friends in bands who would play and break up, play and break up.

True, I couldn't get a job in Detroit. My grandparents left their homes for better opportunities, so why couldn't I? They never talked about the good times in Terre Haute or Buffalo. What was I pining over?

I summarized my case, but Mel wasn't having it. "Pills aren't like weed. You have to get the dosage right."

We found Squeak's burial spot. I plunged the shovel into the ground. The spike into the ground sounded beautiful—more beautiful than anything I'd heard in a long time. But after a few times digging, the act shifted us into a funereal state.

Laura said, "Shouldn't we have a song, or a prayer?"

"Sure," Mel said. We bowed our heads to think. Laura raised a finger and started singing "Ben" by the Jackson 5.

"Oh, very funny," Mel said.

Laura saw something shiny on the ground and bent down. She lifted the end of what was a bracelet. "Told you."

Last spring, she found an engagement ring and a switchblade. I dug a couple more times, noticing Mel's eyes dart between the earth and the baggie. It struck me then: that sense of unrest, of primal dislocation. We were supposed to be someplace else. Laura and Mel were twenty-nine and I was thirty. Our mothers were knee-deep with kids by our age, and heavy into the routine of marriage. And I felt as though some phantom of me had gone onto this other life, and I was too late to follow. It didn't help to call this feeling silly, and I had no place to put it down.

"Here, let me," Mel said. She reached for the shovel.

"Nope," I said. "You have to come up with the memorial speech."

"I think I know what to say." She was a lot better than she used to be, stronger, happier, and it gave me hope.

The dirt was heavy with water. It reminded me that we lived on wetlands, paved over and angry. They haunted us with their steeped dirt that flooded easily and caved the roads every winter.

Mel held Squeak up so she could see. "I can always visit now."

I drove the shovel in again, and it hit with a thud.

"Rock," I said. Every dig, along the side, around the rim, hit hard.

"Ice," Mel said.

Laura said, "Look," and held up a black watch and a dog tag she found. It said, "Pookie." A guy walked by. This wasn't a dangerous neighborhood, but it wasn't safe either. Just some robberies, smash and grabs, and south a few blocks, prostitutes. Urban living, the crimes we'd grown accustomed to.

"Maybe something else is buried down there," Laura said. "Like a casket? Maybe you hit cement shoes?"

"Maybe it's Pookie," Mel said. "Pookie, you down there, fella? We're coming after you."

"Don't make promises," Laura said.

I stepped back and studied my work. "I suppose this is too shallow."

"She'll pop up like a dead goldfish on the first rain," Mel said.

So we walked back to the building with our shovel, the baggie, the watch, and Pookie's tag. We talked about what it would take to melt the ice. A man let us in the building and Laura said thanks. He smiled at Mel, then saw her baggie and walked fast.

Upstairs, Mel put Squeak back in the freezer and lit a cigarette. We collected paper, cardboard, and some charcoals left in a bag at the back of the cupboard. "Okay," Mel said. She exhaled her cigarette smoke, tilted her head to the side, and looked at me with one eye, like a parrot. I knew what she was thinking.

"I'm sorry I got you into this," I said.

"I'm not. I love a good funeral. All that weeping."

We walked down to the basement, where the junk was stored, and grabbed anything we could burn. I found an old metal trash can lid, then headed back to the burial ground. Mel used to work for a veterinarian, and that's where she developed a special affection for animals. For many years, she had thought they were better than people, and sometimes, deep down, I thought she still did. At the site, we squashed the cardboard down in the hole, and then bunched up the newspapers and pitched them in like we were making baskets. We plunked the coals down, about twelve of them, and then Mel took her cigarette end up to the newspaper and said, "Melt the ground and give Squeak a new home."

Laura said, "Careful, your hair." The flame was slow at first, and then ignited in a burst. We were stunned by its wonder. It struck against the mud and dirty snow like a note from a place we had forgotten. Mel stood back.

"The baggie's getting warm," she said.

"Why so quiet, Mary?" Laura asked. She lit another cigarette.

"She's missing home," Mel said.

"Oh," Laura said. We couldn't help but stare into the flames. The coals had caught and glowed, red and jubilant. I didn't wait for a response from Laura. I'd learned by now not to wait for a comment. Why didn't anyone ever say anything here? It made me feel as though people didn't care. You could tell them your best friend died, and they would nod and say, "Oh."

It gave me a sinking feeling that we weren't really friends, just people passing by. Someone told me that Minnesotans never leave, so it was hard to break into their group. I felt this deeply. I'd talked to Meghan about it. She said New Yorkers could be cold, too. "Just paint. The rest will work itself out," she said.

"I'm sorry," Laura said.

"Thanks." Then I was glad for the fire, for giving Mel's pet some peace in this world.

The police car must have come from the alley. The car inched up the road, then paused in the middle of the street. I could see the cops talking it over, trying to figure us out. The driver shook his head, then they pulled over. They eased out of the car, as though they'd had it with the night, their jobs, their wives, and anything else that'd attached to their lives like mussels onto ship hulls. Then we came along, a few pathetic and thin last straws.

"Nice night for a campfire, ladies," the cop said.

The other cop hoisted his belt and said, "Ladies are you aware we have a no burning ordinance in the city?"

I thought that was for summer, but I was in no position to argue. And maybe they would have let us go, given us a warning, but Mel panicked. She gave them the parrot eye, and stepped back. I wanted to say don't. But she thought they'd take Squeak. She slipped the baggie in her coat pocket, and a heavy metal door closed in my chest. In the lengthening list of things one shouldn't do in front of a cop, holding a baggie was bad, but concealing a baggie was criminal. Mel managed both.

"We had to w-w-w—" and Laura went on like a broken record. The cops glanced at one another and then back at Mel. "Warm the ground," Laura said, trying to distract them.

The tall one pointed at Mel. "Ma'am, step away from the others and empty your pockets."

131

"It's not what you think," Mel said.

"You'd be surprised how often we hear that. Empty your pockets, ma'am."

Both cops put their hands on their guns as Mel slipped her hand into her pocket.

Laura dropped her head. Mel pulled out the baggie and opened her mouth to warn him. But the cop said, "Hand it over, ma'am." As the cop put his hand out, his leather creaked. She gave him the baggie. My heart dove. The cop relaxed and he looked at it smartly, as though he'd won something. He put a flashlight on the baggie and his smile doused quickly. He hollered once and short. He dropped the baggie.

Mel yelled, "Squeak!" and went for the rat.

His partner drew his gun and aimed it at Mel and said, "Freeze." Mel did, half bent, as though playing the statue game we knew as kids.

"What is it? What is it?" the other cop yelled. Mel stayed frozen.

"It's a rat," the cop said. "It's a dead rat."

"We just wanted to bury her," I said, trying to offer proof of our sanity. They gave us this look—amazed eyes, mouths wide open—that said we were in a lot of trouble, they just needed a minute to figure out the offense.

The short cop holstered his gun, reached down and tossed the garbage can lid onto the fire, dousing it on impact. Mel went for Squeak again, picked her up, and studied her for damage.

"Step over to the squad car ladies," the cop said, shaking his head, like, *I went to the academy for this*.

They made us walk the line, which was hard around the melting ice. They gave us breathalyzers too, which wasn't supposed to happen, but we were in no position to argue. They took us downtown, and I thought, rather than be upset, this might be another chance to explain our situation.

"See, the rat is Mel's pet," I said.

The driver threw me a dirty look. Laura elbowed me and said, "Shut up, Mary."

We waited downtown while the cops did the paperwork and Squeak thawed. Mel picked up the baggie and frowned at the water collecting in the corners. "Won't be long now, Squeak," she said.

132

They held our shovel, and Laura put the watch she'd found on and said, "It works. Ask me what time it is."

Mel leaned over, "Hey Laura, what time is it?"

"2:30," she said proudly, "a.m."

"Great," I said.

The arrested piled in, crying, screaming; one guy came in without pants and with a coat that just covered his ass. One cop said to another: "Beat this, Clyde. Hooker stole his clothes and his money. So he comes here."

"I'm the victim here," the guy said.

"That's what I like about this job," Clyde said. "The quality people."

The pantless guy, George, wanted to call somebody to come get him.

"He should be in jail," Mel said to us, but George heard.

"Look, I pay my taxes," George said, and he grabbed his coat like he was going to flash us until Clyde told him to knock it off or they'd call his wife.

Our cop finally finished the paperwork. He gave us a $200 ticket for violating the no-burning ordinance, and said, "We're not going to hit you with destruction of public property, or concealing, and may we suggest that you pitch the rat in the trash on the way out to avoid any further trouble?"

Mel gasped in shock at the idea, but he said, "Lady, a dumpster is a rat's paradise."

When the bus finally came, we sat with the shovel, our citation, Squeak, and my guilt.

"I'm sorry," I said, deflated. "This was all my idea."

"I should have given you the pills."

"Well, I think you're both stupid," Laura said. "You should have demanded we meet Tom. We could have racked up a big bill and split."

A drunk guy got on, and sat across from Laura.

"What's your name?" he asked.

"M-m-m-mace is my name," Laura said.

"Ooo," he said. He scratched himself. "A stutterer. I hear they're good in bed. Is that true? Are they good in bed?"

Laura pulled out her mace and pointed it at him. He held his hands up. We rode like that for a while, Laura holding the mace, the drunk guy with his hands in the air. I wondered what we looked like to people, the lit freak show passing by.

We got off the bus and walked to our old fire, where smoke wafted out from under the trash can lid. I got a stick and lifted the lid. The red coals smoldered in the night like grace.

"Why not?" Mel said.

She shoveled once and gave it to me. "It's perfect."

I dug into the ground, heavy with water. I shoveled another foot down until the ground wouldn't give anymore. I was tired. The darkness eased, and the air smelled like an orange. Mel untied the scarf from around her neck and laid it flat on the ground. She set the baggie on the ground and pulled the zip lock open carefully. Mel slid her palm under Squeak and pulled the rat out, as though she were a fine thing that might crumble. She laid Squeak down on the center of the scarf, and folded the soggy sides over neatly, as though wrapping a gift. It was quiet, not a car, not a whir from the freeway. All the sounds were things we didn't say, and Mel's heavy heart, and Squeak still and fragile. Laura and I stepped back, right hands over left, and we watched Mel lean over on her wet knees and put Squeak down. Mel knelt there a minute then got up. We stood close and looked at the little, perfect cloth. I felt the tears on my cheeks.

Mel didn't cry though. She held her chin up.

"I loved you more because you weren't a kitten or a puppy," Mel said. "You were funnier and smarter than all of them. And here I am Squeak, really grateful. You saved my life. I will always remember your pure and funny joy."

"Bye, Squeak," Laura and I said.

"Bye, Squeak," Mel said. Her voice didn't sound sad anymore. She sounded proud.

The night gave in, and the morning light cracked like an egg.

"Now?" I asked.

Mel nodded yes. I took a little mud at first, and slid it slowly off the shovel. Then, when the cloth was buried, I shoveled harder. I took it in mounds, full of anger, out of ideas. When I was done I patted the earth gently and Mel said, "We don't have flowers," so Laura put Pookie's dog tag down like a gravestone.

I studied our work: the little mound and the tag. I wiped the tears away.

I knew life would change for all of us; it was always changing. When I saw Squeak buried, it touched something in me I knew was there for good. It wouldn't fade away with a new place, or the next year. It was the same for Mel and Laura. Life just added up on itself, and then you were you and there was no turning back. I wanted to be proud, to do what made me proud. Your path was your path. I had to accept mine, to cast my dreams within it, because regret or pretending was just beating yourself for believing in something better than survival.

I put my arm around Mel and we walked to the apartment and Mel said, "Thanks for coming, guys." Laura said, "Sure," and I said, "Yeah, anytime."

We walked to the apartment and Mel looked to the swing set a couple of times, as though convincing herself it wasn't a dream, or maybe she thought of Squeak watching the kids play, scampering with her pals, being silly, a mischief of rats running in fairy-tale emergency.

We didn't have to hold onto each other when we walked through the street. The water was slushy and the clouds broke down the middle. What could I say? Spring would come, and kids would screech on the swings. And they would pretend in Technicolor to be barefooted kings and queens slaughtering one another on the warm and busting ground.

We could imagine then that winter never happened, until the first cold wind slapped us and we were surprised all over again, so many lifetimes, it would seem, from now.

# In the Red Room

WHEN MY FATHER and I lifted my sister into the front seat of the Windstar, I understood we'd lost winter. It must have died midway between Thanksgiving and the early days of December, with the acquiescent first shovel of the season, the inaugural whirring sound of the snow blowers. I expected a sudden resurgence—a footfall make-up blizzard—but the storms and ice sloughs stilled, then stiffened, until a few warm days drained those final white patches into the ground.

I didn't notice it until we were in Ferndale, a first-ring suburb of Detroit. I saw the churches and stores decorated for something that felt long past. It was a bizarre moment to expect the white swath of land dolloped with Christmas stars and strings of colored lights, only to find Mary and Joseph figures in front of the Catholic church, staring down at a crib of blown leaves and brown water. Near them, strung to light poles, plastic garland swirled up until their green prongs nearly touched the fixtures. The winds foreshadowed the cold rains, which would fall again against the muddy and hay-colored lawns.

We were together: Meghan and I, with our mother and father. Soon my brother Rob would arrive. Meghan and I were older, and since we left for jobs in other cities, this holiday together meant more to us, those who knew our entire stories, who understood our pitches and doubts.

Our father, with his bad heart, drove us to St. Jude's Hospital. Our mother stayed at home to cook. It was two days before Christmas, and we had already withstood the worst traveling, the meticulous packing of medical equipment, the rush to LaGuardia, and the long lines, thick with people and the smell of greasy sweat. We endured the inconvenienced stewards and the flight into Detroit. Now we had only to drive a few miles to the hospital for blood. Though I'd let Meghan down in other ways, in this new trip we would not, could not, fail.

"You got my phone?" Meghan asked.

I gave her the bag covered in her paints. "Here, in your purse."

"My charger?" Meghan unzipped her bag slowly.

"In the side."

"Meds?"

"Side."

Meghan nodded and closed her eyes briefly before opening them again.

"You're okay," I said, though I didn't know why.

At 9 Mile, she took out a vial of red liquid. At the red light, she pulled off her puffy black glove. That pale hand, once plump from a Midwestern appetite for cheese and an unfortunate side effect of antidepressant medications, had been reduced to an assortment of sticks and knuckles. Meghan lifted her head, cocooned in wool and down, and dropped the liquid on her tongue, as if she were a baby bird, bald and meek, able to feed herself. Dad looked over and seemed relieved. With an innocence I'd envied, he surmised what I had once believed: this was cough syrup for her recent pneumonia.

It was only in New York, a few days ago, that I had glanced at the name on the vial and saw the word. Morphine. Meghan, sensing my distress, studied me from her walker seat. "Can you get me a water?"

I got up, walked to the kitchenette, leaned over the sink, and inhaled the air drifting in from a small window open several inches at the grate. The sink pipes ached as I turned the cold water handle. Water flowing into the home became an amazing concept, the lines of pipe required, the amount of water pumped through to the people in Brooklyn. Where did it all come from? Funny, what we took for granted. I watched the water pour through the filter and rinsed the glass before filling it up and walking back into the main room, so small and covered with books you could barely see the crimson walls behind.

All of that was two days ago. Now, together in the van, I thought we would get through it. Meghan was incredibly resourceful, and having survived this long, with one near-death incident behind her, we could brace together, a seawall against the storm, holding firm until the dull throb of turbulence departed and we could return to our childhood home, sit between the tree and the fire, and turn our backs to this world.

"You're okay," I said again.

I traced my expression back to the rescue dog my husband and I had adopted. The shepherd had been beaten, and in an effort to reassure him, we repeated this phrase.

My father looked at me in the rearview mirror. "Not you," I said.

He snorted and looked at my sister with a bemused expression, *Can you believe her?*

Meghan shook her head and lifted her chin. "She's something."

At the hospital, two valets helped Meghan into a wheelchair. Our father insisted on parking the car himself. Royal Oak was one of those pastoral, Midwestern suburbs with grids of brick houses shaded by thick, red maples and knobby oaks. Amidst such beauty, St. Jude's security system felt unduly muscular.

Five guards stood around a conveyer belt X-ray machine and a walk-through metal detector. Two of the guards helped Meghan stand up, then ran a wand along her body until the beeps could be explained and she was free to pass. I placed her bags onto the conveyer belt, along with my purse. After I passed through the metal detector and collected our belongings, I left the security team to await our father, his pockets full of change and keys.

I walked behind Meghan.

"Mary?" Meghan called out.

"Yeah?"

"We'll have to call Danielle," she said as they wheeled her through the doors. Since we arrived Meghan and I had been planning for her party on the day after Christmas.

"Yes," I said. I'd never seen an emergency waiting area so still and unused.

"When is Rob coming in?" Meghan asked. Rob lived in Utah.

"Tomorrow," I said.

When we entered the emergency room, she grew quiet. We tried to act normal.

Meghan lifted her chin in the air. I focused my stare straight ahead. I hoped the staff didn't gawk at her matchstick limbs and sunken chest.

Under the fluorescent lights, she licked her pale lips. The shadows remained hard and determined against her skin. I practiced what I might say to the nurses. When the aide came to change Meghan into a gown, I said, "We're just here to get blood." The comment came out far too sharply, as though I'd thrown the gauntlet down and stamped my foot in utter disgust rather than set the parameters of the visit.

They weren't nurses after all but aides, two girls just out of high school with bouncing ponytails and clear complexions. They wheeled Meghan into a room. One of them held her palm up to stop me. "We'll change her and bring her out." Then she hit a button. The doors closed in front of me. We didn't want her changed. She could get blood sitting up.

Meghan had told people at her Brooklyn co-op that she couldn't wait to get home for Christmas. She wanted her family, the tree, and the calm.

I was the one who suggested the emergency room. The night before, I sat on the edge of the couch while Meghan watched television. Get blood now, I reasoned, and avoid a Christmas ER visit when the worst cases would line the hallways, bleeding and puking. Her eyes sunk in their sockets. She sipped ice water. I could feel her body tense.

"You're a little listless," I said. I'd promised Meghan then the blood would fortify her, and she would feel revived for the holiday. "We could go now and be home in a few hours."

"I'll think about it." She lay on the couch. On a chair next to Meghan, beads of condensation inched down the plastic cups of Vernors and ice. Her white computer and black cell phone rested against her side.

"I promise they won't check you in. They'll have to kill me first."

She stared at the television, her lips pursed, turning white. Her eye flinched. "I said I'll think about it."

Now, waiting for her to come out in another hospital gown, I wanted to bang on the doors and demand they let her out. For a few seconds I worried they could steal Meghan and not return her. I told myself that was insanity. But it was all insanity, the chemo, the radiation—all of it. When I looked down the halls, no one was there. The walls were painted in pumpkin and vermillion. Someone—a committee or a consultant—must have advised the hospital to paint the emergency area in the calming colors of seasons and nature.

My father shuffled up.

"They're changing her."

He nodded once, and we both faced the doors and waited, as solemn and slouchy as wounded palace guards. When the doors finally pulled back, my father and I shifted to the right, so the women could wheel Meghan through on a thick bed with railings.

"You picked the right time to come," the aide said to Meghan. "We usually get a rush at three, and then after five we're slammed until midnight."

"I see," Meghan said. The aides didn't seem young anymore. One wore a wedding ring. They wheeled Meghan into slit A2.

My father and I stood silently for some time. Meghan fixed her gaze on our father. "Get a chair. Sit down."

He smiled faintly and shuffled on his feet. "I can stand."

Meghan stared at him. It was a commanding gaze.

"Dad," I said. "This could take hours. Don't upset her."

"Yeah," Meghan said. "Don't upset me. Where's my phone?"

"In your bag."

"Will you get it for me? And my charger?"

I plugged in her phone. Then I set it down on the table by the bed, right next to the landline.

A quiet entombed the floor. People walked by, talking evenly. No one screamed in pain. No doctors yelled out commands, and no nurses shouted "Code Red!" as they ran down the hall in their white, gumpy shoes. I needed a life to be saved at that moment. I yearned for the noise of effort.

A woman wheeled past us, flanked by police officers. The woman hit her fist against the bed. She cried, but even this was muffled and quiet.

An athletic, no-nonsense team of nurses and aides walked in and pulled the wheat-and-green curtains shut before one of them asked loudly, "How are you? How do you feel?" The aides were dynamic and upright.

As they got to work—setting up an IV, a monitor, and finding veins— my father left in search of a bathroom.

A nurse said, "Do you have a port? We need to pull off your gown." In seconds, two nurses untied Meghan's gown and pulled away the cloth, exposing her port, and near that, the large lumps protruding along her chest, the malformation of her breast, and the scars from surgery attempts. We told our mother not to come with us for the possibility of this moment, which would scorch her memory forever. A rage ran so deep in my heart I had to turn away. I saw the shadows of people pass behind the curtain. Their movement sent ripples through the fabric.

"I feel weak and need some blood. You need to call my doctor." Meghan took long pauses between her sentences.

I wanted them to leave, all of them, to rush their youthful faces and knowing quiet away from us. What had I done by bringing her here? These were suburban folk. What did they know about our wild-west upbringing in the city, rumbling through in old cars and working two jobs to pay for college? What did they know of New York hospitals and how they always took things: an appendage, a week, a pound of flesh? Meghan went in for a routine infection and left without a breast. When Meghan had reconstructive breast surgery, doctors took too much from the lower belly area, slicing her abdominal muscles. This caused a hernia. She went in with hair and left with none.

"You're okay," I said. I wanted to scoop her up and run from there, run all the way home. I stood still.

The nurse leaned over Meghan. "We'll do that. But first we're going to run some tests."

Meghan's face erupted. Her hairless brows furrowed, and her lips grew tight. Her eyes widened in panic. She was my sister, the girl of long hair and stout build, strong and sturdy. Brooklyn, I called her. She could lift anything. Now Meghan lay under the hospital lights, as bald and bare as a turtle ripped from her shell.

"No tests," I said. I gripped the bed rail.

One nurse, with a maternal nature and layered blonde highlights, took Meghan's hand and smiled in a way that seemed dangerously intimate. "Are you in pain?"

They all stopped. The crinkle from opening plastic bags ceased, as did the clicking and clinking of vials. One of the aides had his back to us. Even after the pause, he worked in slow motion, so he could hear her response. It was as if they wanted to know what it was like, to be so close. Did it hurt? Was it fear or grace? They wanted wisdom, insights they hadn't earned.

They couldn't understand. My sister was a painter and an art therapist—physical, defiant. When you reached Brooklyn via Detroit, you had other stories, ones of yearning, of forging ahead, of seizing and tasting every drop you had left. You fought, with everything, to live.

Meghan's eyes darted. Her shoulders started to lift.

I searched for something logical. "Meghan, do you need pain meds?"

"Please, I need you to call my doctor," Meghan said.

I shuddered. "She's from New York," I explained. "The insurance only covers eighty percent of this."

When they pulled the white blanket over her chest, they exposed the first few inches of her legs. My father heard about the money and slipped back into the room.

The main nurse leaned over the bed and patted Meghan's hand. "You let us help you. That's why we're here."

Meghan rolled her eyes. She turned to me with such a small shift of her head, yet emphatic now, decided. What the hell is this shit?

*Don't yell*, I said with my eyes. *They'll keep you if you yell.* The nurses cleared an area to work and, silently, as if on cue for a part they all played, exited the room to retrieve their needles and vials. I saw the bed with my sister in it and felt ashamed. They only wanted to draw blood, to fill the vials, to arrange the IV. But it was too much. *Just let the tests go, let her retain this little dignity.* I wanted to say all of those things, but it was too late.

My father and I froze and looked at the floor as if we were in church on Good Friday.

Finally, to break the silence, I proclaimed, "You can't get upset. You'll get blood and go home."

Our father sat down in the chair. Meghan looked straight ahead to the curtain and the people behind the curtain, shifting back and forth, causing a small flutter and leaving bits of their conversations with us.

The nurse returned. "We'll draw some blood. They are trying to reach your doctor now. Don't worry."

Meghan closed her eyes. A tear ran down her face. She turned away, facing our father, so the nurse couldn't see. Her pale, soft head, her ravaged arms. How had it come to this? Meghan studied our father's quiet nature, his glum consideration of the linoleum.

"Dad needs a sandwich."

He smiled, his eyes bright and sad. "I'm not hungry."

She kept staring at him.

"Don't be cheap, Dad," I said.

"Yeah." Meghan lifted her head and smiled slightly. "Don't. Be. Cheap."

I looked at Dad, too, suspicious of his slumpy ways. I thought he might fall asleep.

"Is there a cafeteria?" I asked.

"No hospital food. Get him something good somewhere. A turkey and cheese."

"I can't leave," I said.

Meghan turned toward me. The depth of her glare was remarkable. "Dad's here," she said. "You go."

I let go of the bed rail and held out my hand to Dad. "I need ten bucks."

I'd spent thousands traveling from Minneapolis to New York, where I helped Meghan get on her plane to Detroit, so asking for ten dollars felt like a good joke. Plus, it made Meghan smile.

Dad looked at Meghan and shook his head as if to say, *Can you believe her?* He stood up and gave me a twenty. "Get me a coffee, will ya?"

I paused and looked at Meghan. "Do you want anything?"

The bones in her neck and shoulders were made of china now, but her legs were thick and swollen. They glistened. She shook her head.

"Get cream in the coffee," my father said, and yawned.

My sister stared at him. "Sit down."

She turned to me, remembering something. "Where's my phone?"

"Charging. Over there."

"Where's my purse? I need my medicine."

On her legs, I saw fine, thin cracks, with clear fluid dripping out here and there like small tears. My fingers gripped the bed rail again. What was I thinking? The monitors ticked away, the wiring went in, the world swirled around her, and I couldn't leave her to them, not with everything that had already happened, not with what I knew about split seconds in hospitals.

I reconsidered assigning my task to our father, who could use the exercise. I could pull him aside, talk to him in the hall.

Meghan studied me, knowing my plan, refusing it at once with her stare. All her expressions—the girl with the long hair, then a high school teenager who painted, then a college student, so ahead of me, so free, living illegally, painting over on Bagley in rooms now gutted and redesigned as condos—mingled into this one.

"You shouldn't be alone here," I said.

We both looked at Dad. He lifted his shoulders and shrugged. "What?"

"I'm staying," I said. A sandwich was nothing. This time I had vowed to protect her, to keep them from her.

A man came in. "I'm Doctor Cahalin."

We were so dumbfounded. Dr. Cahalin was shorter than me, with a body as round and perfect as an egg. His thinning red hair and upturned nose made me smile, because you didn't see heavy doctors anymore, let alone cute ones. I recognized his black shoes, called LunarEclipse, as the same John wore to run. The doctor's feet were so small I wondered how he didn't tip over. He scratched his head.

"So, I talked to your doctor and everything's set. You'll get blood and go home."

We said nothing. "Are you sure?" Meghan rasped.

Dr. Cahalin stood befuddled in a way that was so sincere, so genuine, it was shocking. He crossed his arms over his prodigious abdomen and rose up on the balls of his feet. "Well, I am the head doctor. I don't make this stuff up."

Meghan nodded. My father watched the floor. My shoulders dropped. In the room, with the beeping monitor and the IV dripping like time, I felt the release of a tension that had gripped the tendons and muscles in my body. I didn't know I'd been holding them up at perpetual attention since the last meeting with the New York doctor. Rob and I listened in the hall as she said, "The average expectancy for stage-four breast cancer is four years." The doctor tilted her head and waited for us to do the math. It had been four years since Meghan had been diagnosed.

The doctor found the acknowledgment in our faces, turned away from us, walked into Meghan's room, clasped her hand, and said, "We'll fight this. Don't worry. We will give this everything we've got."

A week later, that same doctor told Meghan to enter hospice. "There is nothing more I can do."

Meghan wept on the phone then: "She promised to fight with me. She said we were in this together."

Now, Dr. Cahalin turned in his Nikes. "Okay, nice to meet you."

"Thank you," I said.

We didn't say anything until the doctor left. Our father smiled. "Hey, see?"

As the doctor walked down the hall, Meghan's eyes followed him, just like Phoenix, the dog John and I had adopted. The dog had been so badly beaten, he'd almost died. The rescue group gave him the name as a hope. He recovered and learned. But Phoenix still tracked those he feared, in case they betrayed him, because that is what people did. People were shape-shifters. You couldn't trust them. One minute they were nice and petting you, and the next they were drinking from a bottle and kicking you and hitting you with things until you were bloody. One minute they make promises, the next there was nothing else they could do. In the past six months, Meghan had gone into the hospital twice, once for low potassium and once for a blood transfusion. They told her she'd be out by the end of the day. She stayed for two weeks.

I touched Megan's shoulder. "See? You're okay."

Meghan turned her head slowly to our father. She stared at him long and hard.

"This'll take hours."

"Okay," I said, "I'm going."

I found the Windstar, scraped by my father's ill-considered reversals and crooked parking jobs. It sat in the back, under the pines.

As I headed down Woodward, by the bookstore and the OM Macrobiotic Café, the winds of March howled at Christmas. Time went slant. I drove on bare tires through the yellow light and felt myself here, completely, without needing to plan for trips or phone calls. The bad shocks sent me lifting and sinking to Ferndale, which was several miles away, but familiar. I could pull over and call John, but then I would cry, so I kept going.

I saw the road. I wasn't crazy or anything. But things flashed in my mind, so fully and in such a detailed way that they happened at the same time as this moment, like a quantum life playing beside me.

The crossroads came and went, 12 Mile, 11, then 10. Another part of me ran through the moments when Meghan had been diagnosed. The listening, the supportive comments ("You're tougher than cancer" and, "I am sure she's a good doctor"). Then the fights, when Rob and I urged her to stop eating meat and dairy. We told her to drink green juices. She said she would try—but the doctor told her not to eat broccoli, not to eat anything that would interfere with the chemo.

"Okay," I said. I thought, *Look, the doctors are bullshitting you. For God's sakes, Meghan, run for your life.*

147

In the revised version, that was what I said. In my mind, as I drove to get my father a sandwich, that sentence changed time. We were saved.

Months earlier I offered to buy Meghan a juicer. Meghan replied sharply. "Do you know how awful it is to hear this crap? You have no idea what this is like."

Meghan wanted to live. Wasn't it my job to help her live, even when all hope was lost? Even if it were days or months longer? Even before I flew to Brooklyn to pick her up for Christmas, I'd researched a list of restaurants with healthy food. There were three on Seventh Avenue that could make green juice. I wouldn't ask permission. I'd just buy them and stick them in her face. What did it matter now if she got mad?

She'd warned me on the phone: "You know, I look thinner than I did in July." Long pause. "I've lost some weight."

Then I stood outside her door in Park Slope. She buzzed me in. The apartment door was unlocked, so I opened it, already saying, "Hi Meghan."

*Oh no.*

It was beyond weight loss. Her energy had drained from her.

"It's so good to see you." I reached down to hug her as she sat in the walker. "How are you?"

"I'm fine," she said with a worried smile. All the months I wanted her to go to another doctor, to do it my way for once, all that was gone. Now she said, without saying anything, *Tell me I don't look so bad.*

"How are you?" I said again, my hands reaching out to touch her, to cup her hands in mine, to hold her, to be together and weep together and curse the system, the doctors, together. "It's so good to see you." I'd said this already. What was happening to me?

I started blinking. Her smile began to unwind, collapse at the corners. "Can you get me a Boost? And a water?"

I breathed in and set down my bags. "Sure."

I got her a Boost and soon she had more orders, more things to talk about. In a while I recovered, and was so glad to see her. It was better than the worry. Then and there with Meghan, I didn't have to grade papers, and I didn't have to stop grading papers to answer every ring of the phone, just in case Meghan or Rob called with bad news. I didn't have to hang up on computerized messages or tell off telemarketers who pushed internet service, insurance, credit cards, or home loans. I didn't have to look out the windows and see the beautiful day surrendered to packing and planes. I didn't have to feel the tight pain behind my left eye, seizing up. Now, we were together. This much we had.

Now people passed in their Buicks and Escalades, their Suburbans and Land Rovers. I saw an Econoline van and wanted to put my sister and me on top of it in La-Z-Boys so the wind could whip through our hair and we could look out and see the road for miles ahead, take in the clean air. Let people think we were crazy. What use did we have for propriety now? I'd started painting again, and I vowed to paint this piece, as an homage, as a middle finger.

I found a parking spot on 9 Mile, in front of a Buick and behind an Aspire. I fed two quarters into the meter and walked into Al's with the yellow awning where the old wooden floors creaked, and the booths held writers, clicking away on laptops.

Inside, I ordered a beet/carrot/apple/greens juice for me, the coffee, the cream, and the sandwich for our father.

"You from around here?" the man at the counter asked. Above him hung a picture of himself. At the side: another picture of his younger self.

"Yes."

I was from here.

I got back into the car, drove north on Woodward, and sipped my juice. Once I reached the hospital, I thought we should call and invite Johanson, Meghan's painter friend, to our Christmas party. He'd helped get her painting in the president's office at Wayne State University. It was my favorite.

I downed my juice and walked toward the hospital thinking of my sister's painting. It was a little, white image, almost a caricature of a girl, surrounded by a sea of churning red. The valets loped to cars. Someone waddled in like a penguin. I looked to the ground and saw the dull concrete, a puddle, and over there, on the dead lawn, a medical bracelet. I forced myself to lift my head. I breathed in fully and let it out in a huff. The painting was entitled *Figure in Red Room*.

Inside a female security guard held up her hand. "Hold the food as you walk through."

I passed employees laughing at a joke, then a woman in a wheelchair, and another walking down the hall with an IV. The guard had pressed the button, and in a note of perfect timing, the doors separated, and I walked through. *Yes, we would invite Johanson*, I thought. No matter what, we would have the party. That was what Meghan wanted. That much we could do.

It was then that I heard Meghan yelling, "I can't stay here overnight. I won't and I can't. I can't afford it."

I didn't know she could yell. It came out broken and shredded, yet strong.

When I got there Meghan's eyes were full of terror. She looked cornered.

The man near her wore business casual clothes, a striped shirt, Prada slacks, shiny shoes. His back made a prominent V shape, signifying he worked out. He had run mousse through his wet hair, so now it was stiff. He stood back toward the curtains.

"What's happening?" I asked, foolishly clutching my paper bag and my paper cup of coffee.

"They say I have to stay."

I frowned. "The doctor said you could go home."

Our father looked cross and shifted in his seat. "The last time they made her stay overnight she ended up staying for two weeks." He spit it out in a huff, as if his anger had been building for years. "Shit." He pointed his finger out in accusation, a terrible, twisted expression rising up on his face.

Meghan shook her head.

The guy put his palm on me, as if I were the sane one. "I'll double check. I'll see what's going on."

He shot out of there.

*

"Eat your sandwich," Meghan said.

I gave him the bag. He pulled out the turkey and cheese sandwich and tore a bite out of it. Meghan wanted him to eat, so he ate.

As he chewed, Meghan stewed and simmered, almost growling. "I won't stay. They can't make me."

It dawned on me. Of course not. Of course she didn't have to stay. A hospital wasn't a prison, was it? It couldn't keep someone against her will. But she never argued the reasons for staying before. Could she have left then? I thought back. Meghan didn't want to upset her doctor. She had told me after a support group meeting, "If you get your doctor mad, they dump you. It happens all the time."

I looked to Meghan, who held a face of long determination, of practiced resolve. And then I understood her secret. That's why she didn't want the tests. Apart from the money, Meghan knew what the tests would say. Her doctor had told her it was too dangerous to travel for Christmas. Of course the doctor told her not to leave. "You won't survive it." I imagined that's what the New York doctor said. She couldn't be held responsible. But now I knew Meghan and the New York doctor had come to an agreement: get blood or go to a hospital at any sign of a problem. "Don't wait this time. The blood is too important. Have the doctor call me. I'll explain your situation."

Meghan set her gaze on the curtains. She knew I knew. She didn't want to worry us. She could take the news alone. She believed herself to be tougher than us. I leaned over, quiet as a mouse. "In a couple of hours you'll be home by the fire, even if we have to wheel you out of here in this bed."

It was settled. I knew when I got home I'd have champagne, two glasses, and sit by the fire and be with my sister for Christmas.

The patient advocate slipped back in, eyes aghast. "I'm so sorry. That was my mistake. We are not keeping you."

"Thank you," I said.

He explained that Meghan would go home in a few hours, after the blood transfusion was complete.

He put his open palm on me again. I pretended not to see it, because there was only so much we could take without collapsing here ourselves. He left.

"You can't charge me for the tests," Meghan yelled after him. Even though he was gone, she went on about the insurance and how they were all trying to take her money with all of these tests and hospital stays and cab fares.

Dad tore off another chunk of sandwich.

"You're going home today," I said loudly, firmly, so Meghan would quiet down.

But Meghan kept going. "They just wanted to make their damned money, and if they keep me here they'll get more."

"Oh, shut up, woman, for the love of God."

Meghan glared. "You are so *rude*."

"You sound like Dad."

Our father chewed.

"Where's my phone?"

"Dad, where's Meghan's phone?"

"It's plugged into the wall," he said.

"Oh yeah." I'd forgotten. "I thought we should call Johanson."

"He's coming," Meghan said. "What about Danielle and Aunt Joan?"

"We could call them now."

The nurses and assistants came in quietly. One took the blood; the next checked her pulse. The third got the water. The fourth said, "It's time to move you."

Meghan turned to me. "Dad should go home."

I looked at Dad, slumped and sipping his coffee.

"I'm fine."

"Right," I said. "Do you want us to call you?"

Meghan looked up at me. I couldn't believe the blue of her eyes. They were duller in vitality but still so rich and full in color, like the reflection of the noon sun on the lake we knew as kids. "I'll call you."

Silently, I witnessed the understanding in her face. I didn't ask anything more.

Seven hours later, Meghan was home. We had to lift her up the steps and set her back on the couch on top of a deflated air mattress.

152

When she had to get up, we inflated the mattress. That was all that mattered now. She had to be able to get up. We worked constantly. The bathroom, the bag, the Boost, the Vernors, the ice, the water, the fire. The gifts, the time, which passed so fast, as if it were a conveyer we couldn't stop.

Rob came in to town. He hugged Meghan, then they watched television. John arrived that day with the dog. Phoenix came up to sniff Meghan. He wagged his tail.

"Hi," Meghan said with a smile. "Hi."

John wrote the grocery list, drove to the store in our car, bought all the groceries, cooked all of the meals, did all of the dishes, and stayed in the background the way a monk prepares mass. My mother and father held hands on the couch. Rob made jokes and we laughed. He wanted to fix some pipes while he was there. He wanted to fix the cracked window on the French door. The house was three-bedroom brick, solid as mortar, and we were in it.

On Christmas Eve, we all sat around the fire. Meghan's energy rebounded. She ate food near a painting of herself, done by a former teacher. A sip of beer, a bite of ham, some cheese. I drank my champagne—a Veuve Clicquot John had bought that day. I saw the fire and the tree, the Irish saints Meghan had bought as ornaments, and the little Irish hat. I memorized it all, took in every moment. I held John's hand. I petted the dog. Meghan went to bed early. Our mother and father sat close to one another on the couch. We were together. I had to keep telling myself this, so the motors in my mind would slow down. *We are together.*

On Christmas morning, she threw up. It was the food. John and I gave one another gifts in our room. Downstairs we gave Meghan gift cards and a sweater. We walked the dog. We got the Vernors and the water, the Boost, and the ice. We helped her up, and we helped her down. We sat around the tree. We did these things as though we were cartographers, measuring out the details precisely, out of deep regard for the shifting lands. The phone kept ringing. We gave directions. The whole day I took mental pictures. Here is Meghan on the rocking chair. Here is Meghan getting gifts. Here she is, mad that Mom and Dad spent too much. Here she is on the couch.

The day after Christmas, Meghan sat in her rocking chair in front of the fire. When her friends arrived, they bent down to kiss and hug her.

John made pizza at Meghan's request. I walked in to help him. "Be with your sister." He grabbed my hand furtively, as though pulling me to shore. Phoenix and I walked into the living room.

"He's a pretty dog," Johanson said.

"We should get another dog," Danielle added.

"Can you believe this weather?"

"How is your Uncle Tim?"

"Meghan, how is New York?"

Meghan was in a show coming up. She'd sold another painting.

"I'm going to start painting," Rob said. "An hour, a few brush strokes, and you earn a thousand bucks."

We protested, and he laughed. "What?" he said, and shrugged his shoulders.

Meghan sat in her rocking chair with three pillows under her, the fire framing her body. She wore a cherry-tinted sweater. The way it glowed against the fire intensified her pale skin, like the eye of a flame.

The smell of pizza overtook the room, and soon I got up to help John set four of them on the dining room table, along with stiff paper plates, silverware, and wine bottles. Meghan, who loved pizza, sipped water through a straw.

She studied everyone. Danielle talked about her job as a computer consultant. When Johanson downed his wine, Meghan pointed to his glass. I poured more for everyone.

Meghan asked our aunt, "Do you want more food?"

When I saw Meghan then, I thought of things triumphant and misunderstood. I thought of Van Gogh and Theo. I wished Meghan and I had written long letters, private and probing, revealing a love and brilliance. When we read them, the words could have provided comfort in, to use Thoreau's phrase, common hours. I remembered something Meghan had told me. She was in the New York hospital, and I had come to visit.

"Thanks for coming," she had said, watching television. "You are an amazing sister."

"I wish I could do more," I said.

Her head swayed back and forth. "I mean it. I'm really lucky."

I pretended this was nothing, but when I got home that night, I wrote the phrase down so when I doubted the words, they would be there, recorded forever.

Now, in front of the fire, it was strange. Meghan looked like my sister, the one I'd always known. But there was another part of her that seemed aglow, on fire. While the others ate, Meghan's eyes stared vaguely at the Christmas tree, then she asked if people needed more food. We stayed for some time talking. Meghan smiled, and nodded, and wanted people to have more. She bought us all gifts. Calendars with hopeful sayings, philosophy books, and scarves. We had dessert, pumpkin pie. Meghan had a bite.

And then, as if sensing her fatigue, the first guest, Danielle, got up to leave.

I didn't think about this. I'd never considered past this point. Of course they would leave. Of course the party would end. I resisted the urge to whisper, "Don't go. Don't you move."

Danielle looked down at Meghan, and Johanson stood up. Danielle said goodbye first, but waited, in the archway.

"We'll see you soon, Meghan," Johanson said. He gazed down at her with such love, such feeling.

"Yes," she said, looking up like a baby. "See you soon."

The night was coming, they said. Danielle had a long drive. They expected heavy rains.

"How strange," Johanson said with his burly manner. "The day after Christmas."

As I walked them to the door, I resisted holding them back, making them stay all night. "Can't you see what's happening?" I wanted to say. But I got their coats, held the door and said, "Thank you for coming," and made sure it shut behind them.

As they left, I planned the next move. I'd try to convince Meghan to stay at our parents' house. I'd planned it all out. I'd tell her she shouldn't go back, even if she hated me for it. Even if she yelled. If she would do that much, I would stay here as long as I could, until the day before I started teaching again, until the last possible second. Or longer. I'd take a leave, use the Family Leave Act. Let them fire me if they didn't like it. What did jobs matter now? I could feel the heat of my urgency, like our dog in a panic. I could feel the desperation and the futile resolve to stop the machines, to break all the clocks and phones.

Meghan smiled at everyone, and in that smile was love and strain, appreciation and panic, resilience and release. Though the people left, it felt odd, as if she had been slipping out before them, a slow, steady departure. When everyone left, I smiled at Meghan. "That was fun."

"Did they like it?"

"They loved it. They told me so on the way out."

I cleared the plates. In the kitchen, John stopped me. He put his arms around me. I wished for words triumphant or at least palliative. I wished for wisdom that would make the St. Jude's nurses weep.

"She's not okay," I whispered.

He took a deep breath, exhaled, and held me tighter. "No, no she's not."

*Don't go back. Stay with us.* I'd planned to ask this all along. But now, I would not ask. No matter what it meant, when the time came, I would honor whatever she wanted.

My mind clipped on ahead, planning Meghan's move from the chair to the bed. She would need to stop at the bathroom. We would retrieve water, ice, her phone, and a Vernors.

"I'm tired," she said. She got up from the high seat and shuffled with her walker to her bed with the deflated air mattress on top. Rob and I waited until Meghan was situated, then he turned the air pump on, and she rose up as the mattress inflated. Rob threw the covers across her.

I had to sleep. We had only a few days left. I wanted to be there for every moment, every detail. I turned the light off. I said good night.

"Thank you," Meghan called after me.

I walked upstairs to my old bedroom. Rob was in his room, talking on the phone. My mother and father slept. My sister watched television downstairs. I lay down with John, who kissed my hand. "You did it. You got your sister her Christmas."

When the thudding sound came against the wall, I knew it was Meghan. I walked downstairs and proceeded with her string of tasks: a cup of ice, another Vernors, and the remote. I did them silently, without complaint, as if they were prayers on a rosary. Then I found her phone, her computer, her charger, and her medicine.

A loud crack rang out. I ducked. "What was that?"

"Thunder," she responded and pressed the remote.

I pulled back the lace curtain and the vinyl shade and looked outside just as the rain began to fall in torrents, wild sheets of water until the Christmas lights across the road seemed to melt.

"Jeez," Meghan said. I looked over at her, sipping her drink out of a straw. "Good thing we're home."

Within seconds, the streets began to flood. A manger two doors down was pelted so hard I thought it would crack in two or drift away. What powers the sky held. What incomprehensible might.

"Good thing," I said, and with one more glance to the bolting sky, I let the curtain fall.

# Acknowledgments

I WOULD LIKE to thank the Minnesota State Arts Board, the SASE Jerome Foundation, the Loft Mentor Program for support while working on this collection. I am grateful to Molly McCloskey, Alex Keegin, and the late Frank McCourt for their selection of "This is Art" as a winner in Ireland's Fish Short Story Prize contest. I also want to acknowledge the friends, family, and writers who have supported this book, including Mike Gutierres, E.J. Levy, Valerie Miner, Maria Fitzgerald, Jonis Agee, John Colburn, Ed Fraga, LeAnne Howe, Barb Lhota, Ross Pudaloff, Jerry Herron, Mary Elizabeth Ilg, Jennifer Quam, Sue Taylor, Wayne Smith, Julie Gard, Gayla Marty, Kathleen Cleberg, Dale Gregory Anderson, Sherry Hendrick, Maureen Buecking, Jennifer Willoughby, Alexs Pate, Michael Dennis Browne, Jaimy Gordon, Stuart Dybek, Joe Aitken, Bob Aitken, Kevin Miller, Tim Trainor, John Ilg, Patricia Hampl, Cathy Mellett, Keith Hood, and Gary Peter. I am grateful to James Brubaker and the SEMO Press for their dedication and attention. I especially want to thank Jeff Gulick for his tireless support.

Stories from this publication have appeared in the following journals or anthologies: Ireland's *The Bering Strait and Other Stories*, "This is Art"; *The Journal*, "For a Ride"; *Night Train Magazine*, "Scavengers"; *The Penmen Review*, "The Gods of Jackson"; *Prairie Schooner*, "Bigfoot"; *Puerto del Sol*, "Rise"; *The East Coast Literary Review*, "The Ways of Accidents," published as "Stage Three"; *The MacGuffin*, "Squeak"; *Intima*, "In the Red Room"; *Blink Again* (Spout Press), "Roby Burns" and "Tainted."

Printed and bound by PG in the USA